The Adventures of
Ed Tuttle,
Associate Justice

and other stories

The Adventures of
Ed Tuttle,
Associate Justice

and other stories

Jay Wexler

QP Books
New Orleans, Louisiana

Published in 2012 by QP Books.

ISBN 978-1-61027-126-4 (pbk)
ISBN 978-1-61027-127-1 (eBook)

QUID PRO, LLC
5860 Citrus Blvd., Suite D-101
New Orleans, Louisiana 70123
www.qpbooks.com

Publisher's Cataloging-in-Publication

Wexler, Jay.
    The adventures of Ed Tuttle, Associate Justice, and other stories / Jay Wexler.
        p. cm.
    Includes illustrations.

1. Short stories. 2. Fiction—21st century. 3. Judges—U.S. Supreme Court—Fiction.
4. Tuttle, Ed (Fictitious character)—Fiction. I. Wexler, Jay. II. Title.

PS3557.W68R12 2012   813.'53.2—dc22
                                                            2012405727

Cover design © 2012 by David Croy, Chicago, Illinois, *www.davidcroy.com*.

For Walter

Table of Contents

Original Publication Credits

"Black and White Zoo" originally appeared on Eyeshot.com.

"The Adventures of Ed Tuttle, Associate Justice" originally appeared in *Barrelhouse*.

"Lunch Beans" originally appeared on TheGlut.com.

"The Advisor" originally appeared in *Monkeybicycle*.

"The Joy of Shopping for Odds and Ends" and "Horn Incident Report" originally appeared on Opium.com.

"Henry Clay Will Solve Our Problems" and "The Confirmation Hearing of Sonia Sotomayor" originally appeared on McSweeney's Internet Tendency.

"Croquet, Okay" originally appeared on WordRiot.com.

"Eenie, Meenie" originally appeared in *Gator Springs Gazette*.

"Eyes Like Kumquats, Lips Like a Cocked Gun" and "Three Screams" originally appeared on Monkeybicycle.com.

"Embedded" originally appeared in the *Duck and Herring Pocket Field Guide*.

"Reflections on the Distressed Fruit Series, Circa 1952" originally appeared on Pindeldyboz.com.

"What Do You Like Best About Me?" originally appeared on Defenestration.com.

"Clamming Camp" originally appeared on SweetFancyMoses.com.

"The Linear Apartment" originally appeared in *Bullfight*.

"In the Trunk" originally appeared on Hobart.com.

"Methodology" originally appeared in *Cellar Door*.

"E= mc^3" originally appeared in Opium and was reprinted in *The &NOW Awards: The Best Contemporary Writing*.

"You are Not Tu Fu" originally appeared in *Inkpot*.

The Adventures of
Ed Tuttle,
Associate Justice

and other stories

Black and White Zoo

For a very long time now, I have dreamed of opening a black-and-white zoo. In this zoo would only be animals that are both black and white. This zoo would include: zebras, panda bears, penguins, arctic loons, those sheepdogs from the movie Babe, skunks, killer whales, Holstein cows, African swallowtail butterflies, and Dalmatians. Animals that are not both black and white, such as giraffes and canaries, would not be in the zoo.

I had a cat named Splank that was black and white. This cat belonged to my wife before I met my wife, and the cat very much loved my wife and despised me for interfering in their relationship. Because Splank did not like me, she hissed at me very often and bit me and scratched me. Once she scratched my mom in the face and made her bleed. Also, Splank didn't really know how to use the litter box, and she often took dumps on chairs, in plants, and on my books and shoes. In any event, Splank is dead now, so she can't be in the zoo.

Just to clarify, all dogs who are members of the breed of dogs that the dogs in the movie Babe were members of can be in the zoo. Membership, in other words, is not limited to just the specific dogs that acted in that movie.

Some people, when I tell them my idea about the black and white zoo, think that what I mean is that all animals that are either all black or all white can be in the zoo. So, for example, these people think that pumas, which are all black, or polar bears, which are all white, would be in the zoo. These people don't understand anything. For an animal to be in my zoo, it has to be both black and white. Therefore, neither pumas nor polar bears are welcome in my zoo. Or at least they are not welcome as inhabitants. If they want to come to the zoo as visitors, that's fine. But they damned well better pay their entrance fee just like everybody else.

Some people think it is funny to ask me if there will be any nuns in my zoo. You know, because nuns dress in black and white uniforms. When people ask me this, it makes me wish I died as a baby.

Anyways, as a footnote to this discussion regarding my dream of open-ing a black and white zoo, I feel compelled to add that in the many, many years that I have dreamed of opening a black and white zoo, I have not made a single step toward fulfilling this dream. I have, however, climbed Kilimanjaro. No I haven't.

Splank

The Adventures of Ed Tuttle, Associate Justice

I.

E d sits impatiently at the bench's far end, doodling and daydreaming of his impending trip out West. He draws farm animals on his yellow legal pad: first a sheep, then a chicken. Sweat trickles down his back. Even the Court's high-tech air cooling system can't provide relief from the swampy air that has sat on the District like a wet elephant since mid-June. The goddamned high-backed leather chair he has to sit in makes it worse. Several times he has considered asking the carpentry shop downstairs to fashion him a simple director's chair to replace the ornate piece of shit, but he knows the Chief won't allow such a thing anywhere near his courtroom. Also, Ed has to urinate like the proverbial race horse. Since DeLillo felt compelled to read his entire dissent in the *Echo Industries* case from the bench, it's been over an hour since Ed's been able to get to a toilet, and the morning's two venti lattes are now sloshing around dangerously in his bladder. Ed wonders what would happen if he used the anachronistic spittoon at his feet as a makeshift urinal, but just as he begins sketching out a rough pros/cons chart on his cluttered legal pad, the Chief starts wrapping things up. As the gavel falls and the gallery begins chattering about the day's controversial rulings, Ed twirls and sprints behind the curtain, rushes to his chambers, relieves himself in the bathroom there for what seems like forever.

Another term of the United States Supreme Court has ended, and so the Justices, with little or no official duties to perform during the summer, head off for their extended vacations. Some have found boondoggles to occupy them for the season. DeLillo will teach "Introduction to the Common Law" in Venice; Stephenson will deliver a series of endowed lectures at the Sorbonne. Others use the summer to commune with family and friends. Leibowitz is heading to San Francisco for another season of sailing with her kids; Epps and his wife escape to their villa in the Loire Valley to read historical novels and sip Sancerre. But Ed has no real family to commune with. His wife Sarah died some years ago, and his daughter Helen, the prominent Houston chef, is spending the summer honing her craft at a Kaiseki institute in a Kyoto suburb. For years, Ed has gone the boondoggle route himself, giving speeches and running seminars on administrative law, federal court jurisdiction, constitutional adjudication, in Buenos Aires, Hong Kong, Reykjavik. But before long he came to understand the obvious: no matter how exotic the location, working is not the same as taking a vacation. And so this year he has a new plan. He takes off his starchy robe and sweaty shirt, throws on a fresh lavender polo, and grabs his packed bags. A quick farewell to his assistants and law clerks, and then he's off to Dulles to catch his flight to Salt Lake City, ultimate destination Jackson Hole, where he's looking forward to a solo summer of fishing, hiking, communing with nature, everything that's the opposite of his life here, everything he never does.

On the plane, Ed orders a screwdriver, cracks the Zadie Smith novel that Helen gave him for Christmas. He rarely gets recognized outside the Beltway, but he's donned an Idaho State baseball cap, ordered off the internet last week, just in case. As the plane reaches its cruising altitude and the vodka hits his blood stream, Ed lets out an audible sigh of relief, smiles uncontrollably in a surge of near-exhilaration. The term was difficult. He penned too many opinions, is still not sure whether his decisive vote in the year's most publicized case was on target. But it is over and done with now. The pundits and scholars can yelp like coyotes all summer if they want, because the Court is currently thirty thousand feet below him, hundreds of miles behind, and receding. For now, he is just Ed Tuttle, Wyoming vacationer. Ed Tuttle, regular Joe.

It seems like half a day passes before Ed's final plane lands in Jackson. The airport sits within the Grand Teton National Park, and as the tiny craft makes its jarring, nauseating descent toward the runway, Ed peers at the snow capped peaks that seem only an arm's length from his stained window. He's been here once before, with Sarah, nearly twenty years ago, a desperate, ultimately futile attempt to take a week away from the law firm which would make him a partner only a year later. He tried his best, he really did, to pay attention to all the beauty—the landscape's, his wife's—but to no avail. He had appeals pending in several circuits, a summary judgment motion in the works, a petition for certiorari due in a fortnight. Very clearly he recalls floating on the Snake River at daybreak, mentally reorganizing a brief while his wife pointed out a bald eagle, gasped at the forest's splendor. Every time he thinks of this scene—and he's thought of it a lot since planning the vacation a few months ago—he feels like punching himself in the teeth, cracking his own head open with a pair of pliers.

Ed gathers his luggage, rents a car, finds the condo he has rented for the summer. It is a modest unit, located on the south side of the city, about a mile from the town square, near a sparkling new post office, a community baseball field, the fancy supermarket. He plunks his suitcases in the downstairs bedroom and takes a look around the place. To his great amusement he finds that his landlady is some sort of Republican operative. Elephants of all shapes, sizes, and colors decorate the apartment. A frightening oversized picture of Dick Cheney hangs near the kitchen pantry, of all places. Plaques commemorating the landlady's involvement in the state party, her membership in the Daughters of the Revolution, are nailed to the walls of every room. A life-long independent and judicial moderate, Ed chuckles at the notion of spending two months in this lair of the far right. He fills a GOP `96 coffee cup with cold water, sits on the deck, watches the wind blow through the mountain trees, begins planning his summer's activities.

II.

Two mornings later he finds himself once again on the Snake River at daybreak, this time on a cluttered gray rowboat, fly rod in hand, trying to trick unsuspecting cutthroat trout into his guide's waiting net. Jim the guide rows furiously against the current, brings the boat close to the rocky shore where the trout hide and wait for a juicy bug, or bug-like plastic thing, to land on the surface. Ed's line is constantly tangled; Jim must regularly release the anchor and cut the line free, tie up another fly. A few remedial lessons later, however, and Ed is starting to get the feel of the cast. He brings his right arm back gently, not too far, like he is holding a newspaper between his elbow and the side of his torso, pauses ever so slightly at the top of the backswing, then pops the fly forward into the water. Within a half hour he catches something and pulls it promptly, swiftly, out of the current. It is a fish, a colorful fish, a pretty fish, but a small fish. Tiny, actually. Jim traps it in the net, says something about it being slightly bigger than his cigarette lighter, makes a joke about taking a picture of it, lets it back into the river. Ed laughs too, but his spirits are lifted. He figures that at least now he has caught something the size of which he can lie about.

An hour and two slightly larger fish later, Ed starts to tire. He gets careless with his cast, smacks the water with the fly on the backswing, forgets to pause at the top, catches his hat with the fly on its way back to the river. "What's going on back there? Are you fishing or chopping wood?" mocks

Jim. "You know you can't fish inside the boat, right?" Ed's had it. "Can we take a break?" he says. "Isn't it time for lunch?"

Jim pulls the gray boat onto a rocky ledge and sets up a little lunch spread. He's got a small card table, a couple of folding chairs, Gatorade, some grapes, a few pieces of fried chicken, old potato salad. Ed digs in. The chicken is cold, of course, but not too bad, and even the salad is surprisingly edible. He's feeling good, breathing the crisp air, urinating freely into the bushes. This plan is working out nicely, he thinks.

"So, Ed, where are you from?" Jim asks, wiping his face on a piece of paper towel. He's on the youngish side, maybe late twenties, a small goatee, floppy fishing hat like something right out of a, well, right out of a some-thing, Ed figures, but he doesn't quite know what.

"I'm from back east," Ed says through a mouthful of munched up grapes. "Washington."

"Oh, yeah?" Jim says. "Don't get me started about Washington." And then, although Ed makes no effort whatsoever to get him started about Washington, Jim tells a fifteen minute story about how Park Service regu-lations have made it impossible for him to continue leading snowmobile tours into Yellowstone during the winter, which is apparently how he used to make his money during the fly fishing off-season.

"Yeah, that really, umm, really shits the bed," Ed responds, inexpli-cably. It's a phrase his daughter used to use in high school that he's never quite forgotten, though he's not sure he's ever uttered it before.

Jim scrunches up his red, windswept face and looks quizzically at his client. "So, what kind of work do you do out in Washington, Ed?"

"I'm a, uhh, I'm a judge. I adjudicate, umm, disputes."

"Really? A judge, huh? That's a first. I've had a bunch of lawyers on the boat, but I don't think I've ever had a real live judge before. What kind of judge? Traffic court?"

"Ehhh, uhhh," Ed stammers. Back home, people know who he is. Out here, though, it's a different matter. Still, somehow he never imagined that anyone would ever ask him this question, or what he might say in response. "Supreme Court Justice, actually."

"Holy fuck, are you kidding me?" Jim exclaims. "You're pulling my leg, right?"

"No, no. Been on the bench almost a decade now."

"No way. Prove it. You got any ID?"

Ed briefly considers lying by telling Jim that he was lying about being a Justice, but lying has never been his strong suit, so he pulls out his wallet and displays his driver's license and Supreme Court badge. When that isn't enough to satisfy the skeptical guide, Ed pulls out a wrinkled picture of his swearing in ceremony with the President, and this seems to do the trick.

"Tuttle, huh? Ed Tuttle? Aren't you the one who got pulled over for driving under the influence?" Jim asks, referring to the embarrassing situation Epps found himself in a couple of years ago.

"No, no, that wasn't me. I'm the one who refused to recuse himself from the *Echo Industries* case. You know, the big one involving the securities regulation challenge."

"Right, sure," Jim says blankly. "Holy shit, a real live Supreme Court Justice, right here on the boat. Oh, hey, sorry about the language. Won't happen again, Ed. I mean *Your Honor*."

"Really, don't worry about it. It's cool."

Suddenly Jim thrusts his half-eaten drumstick in Ed's direction. "Have my chicken, sir," he offers.

"No thanks," Ed answers. "You keep it."

III.

Back on his porch that evening, reviewing the day's events with a glass of single malt in hand, Ed vows to himself not to reveal his identity during the remainder of his stay. He thinks about what to say if someone asks him who he is, practices several possible answers. He's a firefighter from Kansas City, an editor from Chicago, an insurance salesman from Altoona. Several scotches later, he's a hermaphrodite from Banff, a kaleidoscope manufacturer from Shenzhen. Giggling, he swigs his way through glass number four, then passes out on the patio furniture.

IV.

His resolve lasts about half a day. He is once again on the Snake River, this time on a whitewater raft with a group of others who, like him, have never before felt the thrill of crashing into a swell of crystal water, the spray blasting them in their sun-drenched faces like crisp Halloween slaps. He is in the front of the boat, setting the pace for the other rowers on his side of the raft, following orders from the wiry bearded guide in the back who shouts things like "let's go all forward a few" and "right side back" and "harder, folks, or we're going in the drink." On Ed's immediate left is a pony-tailed girl of some indeterminate high school age whose attempts at demonstrating her sophisticated indifference keep getting interrupted by the exhilarating unpredictability of the outing. At the girl's side, piloting the left side of the boat, is her mother, whom Ed cannot avoid noticing is extremely attractive even in her ill-fitting REI outdoors wear. Like everyone, her hair and face drips with river water, but unlike the others, who all look more or less like drowning gerbils, wearing the Snake has rendered the mom radiant. He finds himself at times missing the guide's orders because he is busy glancing sideways at her and smiling like a goofball half his age. He makes jokes with the teenager as a proxy for talking with her mother, and he even occasionally succeeds in making the girl laugh despite her sincere attempts to remain distant.

When the expedition breaks for lunch at a riverside campsite, Ed grabs a turkey sandwich and takes a seat next to the mom. He learns that her name is Jackie, that she hails from Chicago, that her job involves marketing and some sort of ambiguous telecommunications product or service. Jackie explains that this vacation is part of her plan to spend more time with her daughter Beth, a plan that is only partially motivated, she assures him, by her fear that Beth is becoming too much like her asshole ex-husband Ted, who works as an accountant for some multinational bank headquartered in Geneva. When she asks him about his work, he considers using one of the lines he practiced the night before but can't bring himself to do it. He quietly and in as self-deprecating a manner as he can muster mentions that he sits on the U.S. Supreme Court, and by Jackie's immediate reaction, which includes a slight dropping of the lower jaw and inflating of both eyeballs, he knows he has decided correctly.

V.

It turns out that the road from revealing his identity to enjoying spirited sex in his rented queen sized bed on top of a quilt decorated with salmon-pawing grizzly bears is direct and fairly unproblematic. When it is over, they lie next to each other, hands lightly intertwined, and make hazy small talk. Ed wonders why he hasn't done this more frequently. Only twice has he fallen into bed with anyone since Sarah died, both times with a law school classmate from long ago with whom lovemaking was about as fun as arguing a declaratory judgment motion in a state trial court.

"I can't believe," Jackie whispers, "that I ate an elk steak and did it with a Supreme Court Justice on the same night."

"Which was more memorable?" Ed asks.

"Well, that move you made toward the end there was pretty great," she says, referring to the side twist and buttock holding thrust that his friend Ray taught him how to execute some forty years ago in the beery basement of a Dartmouth frat house, "but the cranberry chutney paired damned nicely with the meat, so I'm not sure."

"Hmmm," Ed mutters.

"And holy shit was that dessert good."

Ed has to agree that the fudge timbale was absurdly delicious, especially next to the glass of thirty year Taylor Fladgate that cost as much as the elk steak itself. In fact, if he was given the choice of having either sex with him or another spoonful of the dessert, he would undoubtedly choose the chocolate, even though he has always found himself somewhat attractive in the inevitable mirror gazing moments, which admittedly have become less frequent over the years.

"Did you bring one of your robes along with you?" Jackie asks.

"What? You need a bathrobe?" answers Ed.

"No, one of your Justice robes."

"You want to know if I brought the robe I wear as a judge on my Wyoming vacation?"

"Yeah. Did you?"

"Like, in case I suddenly had to adjudicate a dispute between a buffalo and a marmot regarding their respective property rights?"

"I don't know, don't you have emergency hearings or something?"

"Umm, no."

"Oh, that's too bad. I thought it might be kind of fun to do it while you wore the robe. Or maybe while I wore the robe. Or both of us. How big is it anyway?"

Ed thinks about the implications, the laundering difficulties. "Well, hmm, no, I don't think that would be a good idea. Not really my thing."

"Just a thought," she says, and then she's asleep.

VI.

He spends one more night with Jackie before she returns home to Chicago, and although there is some attempt at discussing what might "come next," they are both too awash in vodka to make any real headway on the issue. This is perfectly fine with Ed. Indeed, it was exactly what he intended when he put the bottle of Grey Goose in the freezer several hours beforehand. Some mediocre sex follows the martinis, and before either of them knows it, the morning has arrived, leaving no time for anything but the exchange of email addresses and awkward jokes, followed by a halfhearted farewell smooch.

VII.

Several times over the next few weeks, Ed finds himself wishing that he did have his judging robe with him. He figures if he had the damned thing, he would embroider it with a giant purple "S" and wear it around town like a superhero cape, he feels so good about how things are going. After years of storage in his mind's dusty basement, his masculinity has thrown off its cobwebs and made a triumphant return to the stage. He meets his second sweetie pie—her name is Alex—on a ranger-led hike around Jenny Lake. They flirt through wildflowers, support each other's bodies over rocky inclines, make questionable identifications of the native fauna and then congratulate themselves on their efforts. Unlike Jackie, Alex is small, petite even, but a handful. She takes no prisoners, packs a punch. They make love first at her hotel, then in the bathroom of an empty townhouse up for sale that they wander into on a lark on their way home from the rodeo grounds. She is clearly smitten with his position. Women, she mentions several times, tend not to run into men with his particular kind of power on their vacations out West. Ed and Alex stay together for three days, rent kayaks on the lake, float in a balloon over the valley, drink bottles of first growth Bordeaux on a hillside restaurant deck where they watch a herd of elk near a briskly flowing stream. When they part, there are tears, but they do not belong to him. Once again, email contact is guaranteed, future meetings promised. But when he watches her plane disappear beyond the Tetons, he almost immediately forgets what she looks like. Short, he recalls. Tiny, like a gremlin. Pixie-ish.

After Alex leaves, he tries to throw himself back into work. Briefs for the new term's early cases have started piling up, delivered several times a week to his doorstep by a blue-uniformed doe named Brenda not much north of twenty. Curious as to why this non-descript guy in a rented condo keeps getting overstuffed, overnight packages from the Supreme Court of the United States, one Friday afternoon she finally inquires. Soon she is inside at his makeshift dining room table, looking at briefs and memos written by law clerks and staff attorneys, sipping what's left of the Grey Goose and asking endless questions about how he got his job, what it's like to be a Justice, and just what does the Court *do* anyway. When he tells her in response to one of these queries that all lawyers start their arguments before the Court by saying "May it please the Court," she thinks this is the most hilarious thing ever (it's been several straight Gooses by this point), and for the rest of their day together insists on saying "May it Peas and Corn" over and over, which makes Ed want to bash his own head right through the bedroom window. He puts up with it, though, because de-uniformed, Brenda is so outrageously incredibly stunningly gorgeous she makes Jackie and Alex look like Barbara Walters and Condoleezza Rice, respectively.

She leaves about seven that evening, shortly after their second "session" of intercourse (as she puts it), so she can get home and shower before meeting her date—a paragliding instructor—at the Silver Dollar bar in town. When she leaves, like a typhoon gone out to sea, he is not sure what to do. The condo is very quiet, he notices. He pours himself a diet coke for a burst of energy and tries to turn back to the pending cases. He gets through two briefs and a memo, but then can read no more. Instead he opens a beer and turns on a network sitcom that likewise fails to capture his attention, not only because he can't stop thinking about his overwhelmingly crazy luck, but also because the show isn't funny.

VIII.

The next morning, the local radio station has a special guest, an indie singer of some renown named Aileen Kershaw who "burst on the scene" a decade ago with a "blistering fresh sound" and is now touring in support of her new mainstream album that has all the critics crying "sellout." She is in Jackson for three days, playing a single show tonight, a bit of a break in between more taxing stops in Denver and Minneapolis, and she's at the radio station to plug the gig. Ed listens over his morning coffee as he plans his afternoon hike, finds himself captivated by Kershaw's playfulness on air and blown away by the acoustic songs she performs right there in the studio. *Who is this woman*, he wonders. Twenty minutes into the interview, he needs to know more, so he opens up his laptop, closes the "Privileges and Immunities Clause" document that pops up, and embarks on a fact-finding mission. A Google search, some clicks and double-clicks, and pretty soon he's listening to her entire oeuvre and scrolling through concert photos from the late nineties and watching a recent appearance on *Ellen* and thinking that *goddammit, maybe this is love.*

He decides to put off the Rendezvous Mountain hike until after Kershaw has left for Minnesota. Instead, he buys a ticket for the show, spends the rest of the day learning as much as he can about her and trying to figure out what to wear. He discovers that she is divorced; a four year old daughter stays with her dad in New York during the tour. She apparently likes sex quite a lot, particularly of the "Reverse Cowgirl" variety, if one buys what she tells the *Rolling Stone* reporter in an interview from a few years back. He finds a heartening tidbit on one of the many discussion boards he surveys. The thread, entitled "Does Aileen like Older Guys?" reports several sightings of Kershaw not too long ago in Chicago with a musician in his fifties, which is still somewhat younger than Ed but not by much. After a few hours of research, he figures he knows enough about her life history, likes and dislikes, and preferred fruits and vegetables that they could carry on a conversation (and perhaps put together a complicated salad) for hours after the show, which is indeed what he's hoping to do and feels confident of being able to do, given the 3-0 record he's compiled over the previous few weeks.

The clothing issue, however, has him stumped. He thinks about what he might have worn the last time he attended a rock concert—it would have been the Fleetwood Mac show at the Capital Center in Landover, Maryland sometime back in the late seventies—but he draws a blank. In any event, he is pretty sure that nothing in his current wardrobe will suffice. Though he really has no idea what people generally wear to rock shows these days, he's confident that pleated tropical weight brown trousers from Brooks Brothers paired with a pima cotton lavender polo shirt does not constitute the preferred getup. He spends several hours at a nearby shopping center trying on endless shirt-pant-combos. Most are clearly inappropriate for a man of his age and stature. He simply will not be seen, for example, wearing low-slung jeans and a skin-tight, half-silk orange t-shirt. Nothing he wears, moreover, will say "Abercrombie." Finally, he settles on a pair of black Dockers and a gray waffled Henley, figuring the ensemble is perhaps the least noticeable thing he can put together. He finishes it off with a pair of black casual trainers from Timberland, has a turkey club sandwich for dinner at a local restaurant, and then heads to the show.

When he arrives at seven, the time printed on the ticket for the concert to start, the club is nearly empty. He has a Rolling Rock, then another, and a third, so that by the time the opening act comes on—some god-awful threesome from Vancouver playing a mixture of atonal synthesizer and the bongos—he is sporting a nice buzz that makes him feel all is right with the world. When Kershaw finally comes on the stage at around nine, the club is completely filled, and he has to strain his neck over the keyed-up crowd to get a good look at her. She's wearing tight jeans and black boots and some sort of neon pink halter top that stops well short of her waist and nearly makes him faint. She takes the microphone, sweeps some of her thick blonde hair behind an ear, makes some small talk with the crowd before strapping on an acoustic guitar and playing three songs solo while sitting on a stool in the middle of the stage. The crowd is ecstatic, screaming her name, is it possible that Ed sees some young-ish guy throw a pair of boxers at her feet? When the acoustic set is over, she picks up the stool and heads out of view, returning only after the stage lights have brightened somewhat and the rest of the band members have taken their positions. When she reappears, it's with a bright red electric guitar in her hands and a cowboy hat of the same color on her head. A huge smile lights up her face. Ed's too. "All right, then, Jackson," she says, screaming out an E chord on her axe. "I think it's time for some rock and roll music, don't you think?" And then the band launches into the first of many blaring, rollicking tunes that bring the house down.

When the encore has finished, the house lights have come back up, and the crowd has largely made its way toward the exit, Ed tries to figure out how to meet the star. He figures there's really only one possibility, which is to find someone who works at the club and explain who he is and what he wants. At first he hesitates, wondering what the hell he's doing. This is a rock star, for Christ's sake. But then he reminds himself that he too is a star, of sorts. Sure, he may be wearing somewhat inappropriate clothing for the occasion, but he's a goddamned justice on the goddamned Supreme Court, and he's written hundreds of judicial opinions allocating rights and privileges under federal law! Fortified by this thought, and many beers, he makes his way toward the stage where a big guy who looks sort of official is standing and talking to a smaller guy who also sort of looks official.

"Hi, excuse me," Ed begins. "My name is Ed Tuttle, and I'm an associate justice on the U.S. Supreme Court. I'm a big fan of Ms. Kershaw. I wonder if it might be possible to get backstage and meet her."

The big guy stops talking and turns to Ed. "I'm sorry, you're a what? You want to do what?"

Ed pulls out his Supreme Court badge and shows it to the big guy. "I'm a Justice on the U.S. Supreme Court. I was hoping to get a chance to meet Ms. Kershaw."

"Is this about a drug thing?" asks the littler guy. "Are you busting her or something?"

Ed chuckles. "No, I'm not a officer or anything. Well, I'm an officer of the Court, I guess, all lawyers are I suppose, but no, I just am a big fan and wanted to meet the singer. Why, does she do drugs?"

"Do you have a warrant or something?" the big guy adds.

"No, I ... no. Would it be possible to go back stage and just introduce myself?"

The big guy looks back at the smaller guy. Their facial expressions suggest that neither of them quite understands what is happening. On the other hand, neither really has any inclination to object. The smaller man pipes up and points toward a door at the corner of the club. "Just go through that door, take a left down the hallway, and knock on the first door on the right if it's closed. The band should be in there. Good luck. Say hi for me."

"Oh, thanks. Thanks very much," Ed says, and then he pivots on his new sneakers and heads toward and the relevant door. He finds the room where the band is hanging out quite easily. The door is slightly ajar, so he knocks a few times and then pokes his head inside. A bunch of guys are joking around, sipping drinks, playing little doodad ditties on their guitars. She's in the back, drinking a Bud Light and talking with the bass player, a rail-thin guy with a hairdo so bushy Ed thinks it might house several owls. Not sure what exactly to do or say, the Justice pushes the door open and announces his presence. "Hi," he says. "Uhh, hello."

A couple of the guys turn to look at Ed briefly. The presence of a weirdly-dressed old man in the doorway puzzles them, and so they turn back to their conversations and mini-solos. Ed pushes forward. "Excuse me, my name is Ed Tuttle, I'm a Justice on the U.S. Supreme Court, and I was wondering if I could talk to Ms. Kershaw for a minute. I showed my badge to the security team outside, and they let me back here. I'm a big fan."

A sweaty man with a blue and red striped shirt and matching head-band regards Ed suspiciously for a moment, then turns toward the back of the room. "Hey, Aileen, there's a guy here wants to meet you. He says he's a Supreme Court Justice."

In the back of the room, Aileen turns toward the door and takes a pull on the beer. "Oh, yeah?" she says. "Hey there. Order in the Court."

"Hi," Ed says back, taking a step or two into the room. He expects she will come over to meet him, but she takes no action consistent with his theory. "Great show," he adds. "I'm a big fan."

"Terrific," she says. "Thanks. Thanks for coming." She has another swig and then says something Ed can't discern to the guy with the owls in his head. Ed takes a few more steps into the room. A few of the guitar strum-mers look at him with some skepticism. She still makes no move to meet him half way, so he wanders up even closer. He can see the sweat beads on her forehead and bare shoulders. He's practically shaking.

"Hi," Ed says, putting out his hand for a shake. She shakes it, weakly. "I really liked the way you started the show with the, uhh, you know, the non-electric guitar."

"Thanks. It helps me warm up. Plus, I think it creates the right mood." Another swig.

"Yeah, definitely. The crowd...we all loved it."

"Thanks."

"Right."

"So, you're on the Supreme Court?"

"Yeah, been there for a decade almost. Ed Tuttle. I'm one of the quiet ones." It's intended as a joke, but if she gets it she is not letting on. When he thinks about it again during the awkward silence that follows, he realizes it's not actually that good a joke. Or even a clear one.

"That's terrific. That's a really important job."

"Yeah, I guess. So, umm, uhh," Ed mutters. "Do you think by any chance you might have some ... would you have any interest in maybe going out sometime tomorrow or the, uhh, next day? We could talk about music, judging, whatever."

"Oh, hey, no, sorry, I'm busy. I'm actually all booked up for the entire time I'm here. Thanks though. Keep up the good work on the bench. Keep working for our liberties. We have some liberties left, right?"

"Yeah, sure, of course. Hey, are you certain you don't have any time?" Ed queries. "Maybe for lunch or something?"

"No," she says. "I'm really busy the whole time. You know, lots of commitments." The bushy-haired guy chuckles. Aileen smacks him, then takes another drink.

"Oh, well, OK," Ed says, realizing that the whole room is staring at him. When he thinks back to this moment later, it will feel like he stood there for half an hour. In fact, it is only seconds. "I'll see you, then. Good show. Nice to meet you."

"Thanks."

"Right."

He turns and walks toward the door, as quickly as he can without sprinting like an idiot, the eyes of the star and the band burning holes in his back as he goes. From inside the pocket of his new Dockers, he pinches his right inner thigh so hard it will leave a bruise. "It's fifth grade all over again," he says to himself, and can almost feel tears welling up. "Fuck." He exits the room, beelines to the door of the club, emerges into the star-filled, crisp darkness. Finding his car in the parking lot, he unlocks the front door with a bleep of his rental keys, remembers that the Court has just granted review in what could be a landmark telecommunications law case. As he climbs into the seat, he recalls the issue presented, and in a split second sees a dozen fascinating difficulties posed by the controversy. He starts the car, puts it into drive. He can hardly wait to get home and dive right in.

Justice Sam Alito, With Small Green Bunny on his Shoulder

Lunch Beans

T he noon whistle blows, and I put down my drafting equipment. Time for lunch, my favorite time of day. For the past two hours I've been daydreaming about digging into a super-sized bowl of lunch beans, and I have barely been able to concentrate on the blueprints in front of me. I grab the giant wooden spoon that I always keep by the side of my drafting table and head for the cafeteria.

On the way I stop at an office down the hall to pick up my friend Barlow, who also loves lunch beans. "Hey, Barlow," I say, "you ready for lunch?" Barlow, a raging alcoholic who spends most of the day sipping cheap vodka from a thermos he keeps in a desk drawer, is happy to come along. "Oh boy, lunch beans," he says, as he takes a narrow flask from behind the desktop picture of his newborn daughter and puts it in his front pants pocket.

As we walk down the north staircase toward the basement cafeteria, Barlow and I discuss how excited we both feel about eating a huge bowl of hot, steaming lunch beans. It is my view that although I love lunch beans more than Barlow does, Barlow probably needs them more than I do, since his wife just recently died from a massive cardiac arrest. In any event, we've both been eating lunch beans every day since we started at the firm several years ago. I doubt that either of us have ever missed a helping, and holy shit do we love trading lunch beans stories.

When we arrive at the cafeteria, a long lunch line has already formed. Most of the other office workers do not share our gastronomic proclivities, so they are ordering your more typical lunch items like egg salad sandwiches and pastrami. We don't care about this line. We'll wait our turn. I shove my hand into Barlow's pocket and pull out the flask. When I tip the container to my lips, the hot cinnamon schnapps inside burns the back of my throat and gives me a quick and pleasant buzz.

It takes about five minutes, but then we are in the front of the line. The server, as usual, is spewing random quotes from Kierkegaard like they are

SCUD missiles during the first Gulf War. "Dread is the dizziness of freedom," she barks. "Dread is a womanish debility in which freedom swoons!"

"Hey, Bella," I say. "What's happening?"

"The individual in dread of being regarded as guilty becomes guilty," she responds. "So, what can I get you two for lunch today? The usual?"

I pat the top of my chin with a handkerchief to wipe away the drool that has welled up there in anticipation of the heaping bowl of lunch beans I will soon have before me, and I hold out Barlow's flask for Bella to take a sip from. "That's right," I say. "Two large bowls of lunch beans, please."

Bella grabs the flask and takes a gulp. This woman is something else. It is widely understood among those who follow such matters that she took her degree in the sciences from a consortium of major universities back in the early fifties without ever taking an essay-based final examination but never sought to publish her honors thesis. Nonetheless, her travels in the Northern Baltic States are legendary in certain circles, and the fictional account of those adventures either did or did not win several Booker Prizes. Moreover, her groundbreaking anthropological work with numerous unnamed rhinoceros hunting communities in some place or other was the inspiration for at least three groundbreaking monographs written by minor disciples of Einstein in the mid-sixties. In spite of all this, she took the job here in the cafeteria three years ago to, as she puts it, "be among the people," and also because somewhere in the interim she went totally fucking insane.

"All right boys, two bowls of lunch beans coming up," she says, taking another belt from the flask and then returning it to me. A moment passes in which I lick my wooden spoon in unabashed eagerness, and that's when Bella speaks a certain set of words which sends the world spinning in a slightly different direction.

"Looks like there's only enough lunch beans for one bowl today, fellas. In the possibility of dread freedom succumbs. Can I maybe get one of you an egg salad sandwich or something?"

"Only enough lunch beans for one, you say?" Barlow inquires, clearly startled by the news.

"I've got hedgehogs in my swimming trunks," Bella responds inexplicably.

Barlow turns to me in a near panic. "Jesus Christ, what the hell are we gonna do, Zweiffach?" he asks. The man is starting to freak out, you can tell. His ears are turning a bright shade of red, and his nose is running. "They only got one bowl. Only one bowl!"

"All right, all right, calm down, we can handle this," I say, trying to bring Barlow back to earth. I'm acting relaxed about what's happening, but inside I'm as frazzled as he is. Only enough for one bowl? What the hell *are* we gonna do?

"My wife is dead, man. She's dead," Barlow exclaims.

"I know, Barlow, I know. Dear lord, I know."

"She had a wicked liver infection," he adds.

"Cardiac arrest," I correct him. "Massive one."

"Right. Anyways, she's dead as hell. And if I don't get a healthy helping of lunch beans, I'm not going to make it through the day. I'm just not going to make it."

I hand the flask back to Barlow. "Now let me think about this for a minute," I say, and then I begin to give the problem some thought. As I see it, we have several options. On the one hand, we could choose a solution that would put us both on the same footing. Under this approach, we could either both eat half a bowl, or we could both order an egg salad sandwich. On the other hand, we could figure out some contest or something where the winner gets the whole bowl of lunch beans and the loser takes the egg salad. But what kind of a contest is suitable for determining which of two co-workers gets a bowl of lunch beans? And who is qualified to judge such a contest? I consider these questions at length. The rest of the line is getting restless. I can tell they're getting restless because people start screaming and yelling at us to hurry up. "Let's get a move on," demands a gray-suited bureaucrat. "Hurry the fuck up," screeches a pig-tailed librarian.

The issues are difficult, and I'm not sure what to do. It's true that Barlow needs these beans. He has gone through a lot. Looking at his tear-stained face and quivering hands now, I can tell that Barlow is really hurting inside. On the other hand, it's not like I haven't had my own share of disappointments in this life. I mean, just last week I experienced some minor difficulty when wiring up the new sixty-two inch plasma television that my wife, the Duchess, bought me to celebrate the sale of my first screenplay. And then there was the time last winter when my Jaguar XJ6 didn't start on the first try. No, Barlow owns no monopoly on worldly suffering. And the thought of a day without those juicy, steamy lunch beans is almost too much to bear.

When I see Griswold, our bespectacled supervisor, enter the cafeteria, I suddenly know exactly what to do. "Jesus Christ, Barlow," I say in a voice loud enough for everybody in the cafeteria to hear, "for the last time, I will not get drunk with you during working hours."

"What? Huh? What are you talking about," Barlow asks, practically whimpering. "What does this have to do with lunch beans?"

I raise my voice even higher. "Look, you irresponsible drunk, I won't countenance any more drinking on company time. Now put that flask away before I report you to Griswold!"

Barlow starts waving the flask around willy-nilly in the air. "Why are you saying this to me?" he squeals. "Why are you doing this?"

By now, Griswold is on his way over, and I can tell he's completely buying my act. Griswold hasn't been happy with Barlow's work for a long time now, and he has been looking for any excuse to send Barlow packing. Plus, it was during vigorous sex with Griswold that Barlow's wife suffered her massive coronary, and ever since, the mere sight of Barlow, not to mention that picture of Griswold's kid on Barlow's desk, has been enough to make Griswold feel sick with shame. Getting rid of Barlow would make Griswold's life at the office much less psychologically difficult.

"Is this true?" Griswold says, approaching us and grabbing Barlow by the lapel. "Have you been drinking on the job?"

"Well, yeah, I guess. But, I, uhh, well, umm, I want lunch beans?" Barlow says pathetically.

"All right, let's go," Griswold says, pulling Barlow out of the line and toward the cafeteria exit. "We've got a lot of paperwork relating to your discharge to get through this afternoon, and I've got Knicks tickets for tonight so we can't dilly dally."

With Barlow gone from the line, nothing can stop me now. "One bowl of lunch beans, please," I say. Bella, who never much cared for Barlow anyway, cracks a giant smile. "You are one dreadful man, Zweiffach," she giggles. "One dreadful, lunch-bean-loving little man." She scoops me out a heaping, steaming bowl, and I dig in before taking even one step toward the cashier.

The Advisor

It began with an odd conversation about Confucius. I had been volunteering at the "Robertson for President" campaign headquarters for several months, doing strange things like making phone calls to potential voters in places like Iowa and Arizona, stuffing envelopes, entering data into spreadsheets, that sort of thing, but I hadn't met the actual candidate—Tom Robertson—until one afternoon when he made a rare appearance at headquarters to give the staff a little morale boost. The primary season had begun in earnest, and the candidate was doing well, but the staff had been working hard for a long time, and it was the middle of winter, and success was far from assured. Robertson came by to explain why he was the only Democratic candidate that could possibly beat Montgomery, the Republican incumbent, and Robertson, in his typically inspiring way, urged all of the staff members and volunteers to keep on fighting, not to give up, to stay strong for the future of America, despite the seemingly endless barrage of snow and the uncertain vicissitudes of politics.

Anyway, Confucius. After giving his truly rousing address to the fifty or so of us who had made it to headquarters that day, Robertson made a point of trying to talk at least a bit to each and every one of us during the sort-of impromptu Coke and potato chip reception that followed. It was a magnanimous gesture, and one that we all appreciated. Pretty much the candidate asked us about various details of our lives: where we were from, whether we had families, what other things we were doing with our lives, that sort of thing. When he came around to me, I explained how I was a law student and that I wanted to practice international law after I finished school. He asked me why I would want to do that, which caused me to mention that I had lived in China for a couple of years before going to law school and that I had been an Asian Studies major in college. I had no idea that revealing these innocuous details was to have such an impact on the man.

"Asian studies, huh?" Robertson said. "You do a senior thesis?"

"Yeah, I guess," I answered, remembering with some dismay the complete mediocrity of that piece of work.

"What was the topic?"

"It was basically about Confucius."

"Confucius!" the candidate exclaimed. "Is that right? I've been reading a lot of Confucius lately. There's some stuff in the *Analects* there that has really got me intrigued. Mind if I ask you a question or two about it?"

"Umm, well, sure," I said, taken aback by the candidate's reaction.

"Great. I've got one of the passages that is giving me trouble right here." Robertson dug his fingers deep into one of the back pockets of his suit pants and pulled out a couple of pages of rumpled paper. He flattened the pages out on a nearby desk and motioned for me to take a look at them. Alas, they were pages that had been torn out of a copy of the Confucian *Analects*, and they were covered with handmade scrawlings, scribbles, and margin notes of various shapes, sizes, and colors of ink. A red "Splendid! Loyalty as Epiphenomenon!" at the top of one of the pages immediately caught my eye.

"What the hell is going on in this passage, Judson?" he asked me, putting his heavy arm around my shoulder and pulling me down towards the desk. He was an enormous man who had played many years of professional hockey before entering politics, and his weight bore down on me like a truck. He pointed with a thick finger to a passage in the middle of one of the pages. "I mean, this thing here. What's up with this?"

I looked at the passage closely. It was from Book XII of the *Analects*: "The virtue of the gentleman is like wind; the virtue of the small man is like grass. Let the wind blow over the grass and it is sure to bend." It's one of the classic passages. It means that the leader must lead by moral example. If he is upright, then the subjects will be upright as well. I explained this to Robertson. I kept it brief. I couldn't believe he really wanted me to explain to him a passage from the Confucian *Analects*.

"Really, is that it?" Robertson answered, seemingly startled by my explanation. "I thought it was about how there are some people who are right, and some people who are wrong, and that if a person who is right just speaks his mind to a person who is wrong, the person who is wrong will realize how wrong he is and admit that he is stupid. I thought, you know, that like if I was in a televised debate with Montgomery, and I explained why his idea to privatize Medicare is asinine, then he would see where I was coming from and admit that I was right and he was wrong. You know, like right there on TV."

I paused and looked at him for a few brief moments. Was he serious? "No, that's not it," I said.

"Well, shit, that's good to know, kid. I'm glad I ran into you." He took out a green pen from his jacket pocket and scribbled something on the crumpled page. Then he shoved the pages back into his pants pocket. "Hey, I gotta take off now to a chicken dinner fundraiser over in West Pleasant, but would you mind if I took down your number so I could give you a call if something else comes up?"

"Uhh, sure," I said.

"Great."

And so I told him my number. He wrote it on the palm of his hand with the green pen, and then he left.

That night, back in my apartment, alone with my wife Ellen, eating a concoction of hers we like to call "Tamale Pie," I told her the story of my encounter with the candidate. Ellen, who is officially an "independent," had supported Montgomery ever since he first announced his candidacy over five years ago. My story just made Ellen surer in her conviction that Tom Robertson was a lunatic who didn't stand a chance of ousting the incumbent come November.

"The Confucian *Analects*?" she asked. "Loyalty as epiphenomenon? Are you kidding?"

I tried to tell her that at least Robertson was interested in ideas, that he had read widely in the sacred texts of diverse cultures, that this curiosity and intellectual seriousness meant that he was a man of integrity, a man that could be trusted with responsibility, a man capable of leading a pluralistic nation through tough challenges. By contrast, I pointed out, Montgomery probably couldn't locate China on a map. He wouldn't recognize the Confucian *Analects* if they bit him on the ass and called him Sheila.

"A green pen?" she said, skeptically, shoveling a spoonful of pie into her mouth. "He wrote your number on his hand? Jesus Christ!"

There was nothing I could say.

Two weeks passed without hearing anything from Robertson. I went on with my life, studying for my classes, volunteering at campaign headquarters, entering my prize Bonsai trees in regional competitions, that sort of thing. Super Tuesday was coming up soon, and Robertson was in a tight two man race for the nomination with Randy Barron, who was making quite a showing in some of the southern states. One Tuesday night, while Ellen was at her weekly iyengar yoga class, I was looking over my Criminal Procedure casebook when the phone rang. Usually I let the machine pick it up, but I was bored of reading about illegal searches and seizures, so I got the phone myself. It was Robertson.

"Judson, is that you, you old dog?" was how he started up the conversation.

"Why, yes, sir. How are you tonight?" I responded, suppressing the urge to say "woof woof." "Where are you? What are you up to?"

"Oh, I don't know," he said. "Somewhere in Ohio I guess."

"Another chicken fundraiser?" I asked.

"No. Salmon this time. You know, heart healthy. Salmon, the new chicken."

"Yeah."

"Look, anyways, Judson, I gotta go give a keynote address in a couple of minutes, but I wanted to ask you a quick question about something. You did say that you took some political philosophy classes out there at Swarthmore, didn't you?"

Political philosophy? Swarthmore? "Umm, well, I dabbled a little in the political philosophy, sure," I lied. My roommate at Penn State was a political science major, and he talked a lot, so I figured perhaps I could fake it. "What's on your mind, sir?"

"I've been having a lot of trouble with this Xenophon I've been looking at."

"Ahh, yes, Xenophon," I said.

"It's really tricky shit, Judson."

"That's the thing about Xenophon," I agreed, never having heard of Xenophon before in my life. Was this a person? A book? A musical instrument? "Tricky, tricky."

"Here's my question for you. I've been reading the *Memorabilia,* you know, where Xenophon argues that the essence of human virtue is dependent upon an anthropogenic principle of mind-body interspatiality that is consistent with a eudaemonistic reconciliation of the soul with the four humors...."

"Oh, sure, who could forget that classic discussion?" I interjected, thankful at least to know that this Xenophon was a person. Unless maybe he was some sort of talking horse. Or a fish!

"Right. Anyway, I'm having a hard time getting my head around how all this affects the ongoing debates about health care policy and other forms of government subsidized social welfare. What do you think about that, Judson?"

"Umm, great question," I said, now scouring the living room bookshelves for some volume that might possibly give me something to say on the topic.

Luckily, he couldn't help offering some of his own thoughts on the matter. "I mean, on the one hand, the idea of virtue as something uniquely located in the human soul does seem to justify an interventionist role for government with respect to social welfare policy, but on the other hand, this Xenophon, well, you know, he's a bit of a clown. Sure he says that he's a natural law theorist, but I'm not sure he even places much stock in natural law theory!"

"Right, yes, I see the dilemma," I said, trying to think of how I could buy a little time. "Very difficult matter. Could go either way on this. Indications point in different directions. Real hermeneutical challenge."

"Oh, hell," he fortunately interrupted. "They're introducing me for my keynote address. I'm gonna have to go. But hey look, could you give this matter some thought and then shoot me an email with your views? I could really benefit from your thinking here."

"Sure," I said, still confused by the man's interest in my opinions. "Be happy to."

"Terrific. And if I could get something on you from this by tomorrow COB, that'd be great. I've gotta speak to the IBEW tomorrow night in Des Moines, and I'd like to use some Xenophonian theory to address pending matters with regard to collective bargaining, airline deregulation, etc."

"Oh, of course you would," I said. "I'll get right on it."

"Thanks."

"Cheery-o, then," I said, like an idiot, but he had already hung up.

I spent most of the next day at the library, researching Xenophon the best I could. I quickly realized that Xenophon was indeed not a talking fish but a Greek historian and philosopher, circa 400 B.C., and a companion of Socrates, about whom most of his writing, when it wasn't dealing with horsemanship (really!) centered. I took all of the primary sources that I could from the shelves, along with a selection of what seemed to be the best secondary sources, and I set about trying to find something useful to say on the question Robertson had asked me. I started my work at about 9:00 a.m., and by about 10:30 or so I had come to the conclusion that Robertson didn't know the first goddamned thing about Xenophon.

I mean, the mistake about Confucius was one thing. Anyone can misread a passage. But this was something else. There was not a shred in the *Memorabilia*, which is basically a record of Xenophon's memories of Socrates, that had anything to do with what Robertson was talking about. I read that book twice, and then I breezed through the other books, in case Robertson had gotten the name of the book he was thinking of wrong, and then I read through all the secondary literature I could find, and at the end of it all I was convinced that Robertson was just wrong. The *Memorabilia* simply did not say that the essence of human virtue is dependent upon an anthropogenic principle of mind-body interspatiality that is consistent with a eudaemonistic reconciliation of the soul with the four humors. But how was I to tell Robertson this?

I had to "shoot" Robertson an email by five o'clock, so I had little time to think of a plan. One possibility was to pretend that Robertson had gotten Xenophon right, and then to come up with some argument linking his "interpretation" to social welfare policy. But that seemed disingenuous. Instead, I decided to endorse the other side of Robertson's dilemma: that Xenophon was a clown who wasn't to be trusted, an argument that seemed from my reading to be at least plausible. By doing this, I avoided getting into Robertson's flawed reading of the text, while still providing some advice based on my research. I wasn't sure the strategy would work, but I had no other options. I drafted up the email, suggested that Robertson ignore Xenophon entirely when considering issues of social welfare policy, and clicked "Send" at about 4:59. Then I went home to watch C-SPAN.

Ellen was busy running through her yoga exercises in the living room, so I turned on the set in the den. I cracked open a bottle of hard cider and prepared to watch Robertson's IBEW speech. I hadn't done any reading for my classes the next day, but so what? I was involved in a presidential campaign now, providing high level advice to a legitimate presidential candidate. Sure, the advice was about an obscure ancient Greek historian whose works had nothing relevant to say about the modern world, and sure it appeared that the candidate couldn't understand a philosophical passage to save his life, but what did I care? I was in the thick of things, and for a twenty-six year old this was really heady stuff. I turned up the volume when Robertson took the stage.

For the most part, Robertson's remarks were typical stump speech stuff—critiques of the incumbent's policies, reasons not to vote for the other challengers, promises to improve job security, that sort of thing—and the audience seemed really impressed with the candidate's message. But toward the end of the speech, Robertson's sudden invocation of Xenophonian theory appeared to catch most, if not all, of the attendees somewhat off guard. "And not only must we turn the economy around," Robertson announced, "but we must always remember Xenophon's message that the essence of human virtue is dependent upon an anthropogenic principle of mind-body interspatiality that is consistent with a eudaemonistic reconciliation of the soul with the four humors."

"*But Xenophon never even said that*," I screeched at the television.

"And with this message in mind, we must redouble our efforts to promote government sponsored welfare programs, including most importantly subsidization of certain yet-to-be-officially-proposed alternative medicine programs focusing on at least two or three of the most prominent humors, whatever those may be."

"Aw, Jesus," I yelped, throwing my half drunk bottle of cider down onto the rug. What the fuck was he talking about?

The silence in the auditorium was painful, even thousands of miles away watching it on television, but soon enough, after a couple more inexplicable sentences about the mediocre Greek historian, the candidate returned to his core message: jobs, the economy, health care, taxes, and national security. The audience seemed to release a collective sigh of relief. When the speech was over, the several hundred politically active electricians who had come out for the event engaged in the familiar post-campaign speech activities of applauding, shouting, and chanting catchy slogans in a coordinated fashion.

I too let out a sigh of relief, at least for Robertson's sanity and possible political future, but I was also worried about the inaccurate representation of Xenophon's thought, not only because it reflected badly on the candidate, but also because it suggested that he had not been persuaded by my argument. I mean, maybe I had gone too far when I wrote that Xenophon was a "washed up, good for nothing, second rate blowhard of a historian whose reflections on the good life weren't worth the price of the papyrus they were written on!!!!!" The only conclusion I could draw was that Robertson read my message but decided to ignore my opinion. Probably he was mad at me for not taking Xenophon seriously enough. I figured my days as high level presidential candidate advisor had come to an end.

The next few days passed like a river of thick sludge. I waited for the phone to ring, checked my email every ten minutes or so, but received no word from Robertson. Too depressed even to put on pants, I skipped classes and even failed to attend the monthly meeting of my Bonsai club, at which I was scheduled to make a multi-media presentation on "Wintering Juniper Bonsai in Extreme Climates: Some Preliminary Thoughts and Prescriptions for Future Research." When the president of the club called to see how I was doing, I mumbled something about having rubella and then stopped talking. Fifteen minutes later, Ellen popped in wearing a Robin Hood style feathered cap and canary yellow angora leg warmers. She looked at me quizzically and then hung up the incessantly beeping telephone.

"Jesus Christ, what the hell is the matter with you?" she asked.

"No trousers," I answered.

"You're pathetic," she said, walking out the door.

Several days later, Ellen and I were sitting at the kitchen table eating her special tangy version of turkey tetrazzini when we heard a loud knock at the front door. "Who could be knocking at the door at two in the morning?" Ellen asked. Grabbing the loaded twenty gauge shotgun we keep by the stove for just such occasions, I went to check.

Incredibly, it was Robertson. Dressed in a rumpled gray suit, Robertson stood on our front stoop whistling an old Neil Young tune and stroking a soft white kitten that he was holding in his gigantic muscular arms.

"Robertson," I exclaimed. "I didn't know you liked Neil Young."

"Hey there ol' dog," he answered, ignoring the whole Neil Young matter. "I was just in the neighborhood and thought I'd drop by, shoot the shit, you know."

"Yeah, sure. Why don't you come in. Let me take your coat."

"Umm, OK," he said. "But would you mind not pointing that twenty gauge shotgun at my face?"

I put the gun away and then hung Robertson's suit jacket in the hall closet. When I turned around to lead Robertson to the kitchen, I found him kneeling on the floor and talking to the kitten in a sing-songy voice that made him sound like a seven year old Swedish girl.

"Hello, kitty kitty. Who's a good kitty? You're a good kitty. Goooood kiiiiiittty."

"My wife and I were just having some turkey tetrazzini in the kitchen if you'd like to come in and join us," I said.

"That's a gooooood kitttty," Robertson sang. "Who's a special kitty kat? Gooood kittykittykittykittykitty."

I waited there for about three minutes while Robertson cooed to his kitty and then, not knowing what else to do, I stepped past him and into the kitchen, where I explained the situation to Ellen. Then we talked about our plans for an upcoming vacation in Costa Rica for the next twenty minutes, until finally Robertson came trudging into the kitchen, catless, and took a seat at the table.

"Got any beer?" he asked.

I retrieved a Sam Adams from the refrigerator and introduced Robertson to my wife. "This is Ellen. She supports Montgomery," I said.

"Oh yeah?" said Robertson, taking a long slug from the bottle. "Well, he'll probably get another four years."

"How can you say that?" I asked. "You're going to kick his ass in November."

"I don't even think I'm going to make it to November, Judson. Barron's going to crush me on Super Tuesday and that's going to be the end of the campaign. That guy just understands the voters better than I do. He knows, for example, what they want, or whatever."

"But you understand what the voters want, Robertson," I responded.

"No, no. I don't know anything about voters. They're all mysteries to me. I'll never understand their needs and wants and curiosities. For all I know about how to connect with the electorate, I might as well be giving speeches to a bunch of oak trees. Or lollipops."

I didn't know what to say, so I was quiet. We were all quiet. Robertson finished his beer, placed the bottle deliberately down on the table top, and sighed. Ellen and I looked at each other and shrugged.

"Oh, fucking A," exclaimed the candidate, and then he put his head straight down on the table and sighed again.

Even Ellen, not one easily moved by run-of-the-mill signs of severe emotional distress, was touched by the candidate's glumness. "Oh, please. For god's sake, you have to perk up," she demanded. "Listen, do you want to make some cookies? Whenever I feel down in the dumps I bake a batch of cookies and I always feel better. Why don't we make some cookies? Do you want to make cookies?"

"Yeah, Robertson," I added. "Make cookies."

Robertson mulled it over. "Perhaps you're right," he said. "Maybe I should make cookies. Anyone got an apron?"

"I do," I chirped.

Robertson dove headlong into the cookie baking task. With Ellen at his side and a Mrs. Fields cookie cookbook laid flat on the countertop, he sifted flour, measured baking powder, chopped walnuts, melted butter, and mixed everything together with such gusto and relish I was reminded of stories my mother used to tell me about Julia Child in her prime. It was like watching the Tasmanian Devil or something, except that instead of wreaking havoc around the countryside, this little demon was baking a delicious confectionary treat right there in my kitchen.

When the cookies were finally in the oven, and the sweet, rich smell of "chocolate nutty coconut drops" had filled the room, Robertson seemed to be in better spirits, so I tried to turn the conversation back to the campaign. "Hey, Robertson, do you have any more research projects you want me to do?" I asked.

"Oh, yeah, right, yeah," he said, fumbling around in his pockets. "I wrote up a little list of questions that were kind of bugging me. You know, stuff that popped up while I was on the campaign trail. They might not end up mattering or anything, but maybe you can look into them. Who knows, something might come up in a debate or be useful for my concession speech or what have you."

After a bit more searching, Robertson pulled out a crumpled piece of notebook paper from his inside jacket pocket and flicked it at me. I caught it, and while he went to the refrigerator to get another beer and Ellen peeked into the oven to check on the baking cookies, I smoothed the paper out and took a look. A heading scrawled in red ink declared "Questions To Help Communicate More Cogently To The American People, While Addressing The Important Issue Of The Continuity Of Thought And Relating Intellectual Currents To Concrete Such And Suches," and underneath was a list of questions. I scanned the list. It was long. There were maybe twenty questions, and many of them had several subparts. "What are the implications of Marsilius of Padua's conception of populism for the Green Party's critique of the inheritance tax rollback?" "Does Hume's notion of causation cast doubt on statistical studies demonstrating only minimal correlation between domestic citrus fruit grove subsidies and trade policy on the Indian Subcontinent?" "What role, if any, should Maimonides' theory of human perfection play in formation of American food stamp directives with respect to certain of the larger Great Plains states? The Eastern Seaboard?" Jesus Christ, I thought. Was this really the price I had to pay to be involved in a presidential campaign?

I was on the verge of telling Robertson that I didn't think focusing on antiquated philosophers was going to help him in the primaries when the candidate suddenly started freaking out about his cat.

"Squeaky!" Robertson screamed. "Where's my little Squeaky?!"

By the time Ellen and I had realized what was happening, Robertson was well on his way to turning our apartment into something resembling the Iraqi National Art Museum after the fall of Saddam. The candidate was ransacking the place, tossing pillows and blankets off the bed, rifling through drawers, pawing around in the medicine cabinets, lifting up (and not putting back down) toilet seats, removing pictures from the wall, overturning coffee tables and other large pieces of furniture, going through our mail, that sort of thing, all the while calling desperately for his cat to return to the safe comfort of his beefy arms. "Squeaky, Squeaky," he cried, repeatedly. We tried to calm the man down, to stop him from decimating our home, but we honestly had no idea what to do. We could have tried to forcibly stop him, perhaps by sitting on him or firing a bullet at his leg, but we were physically no match for the three time winner of the NHL's Hart Trophy and neither of us were much inclined to shoot anyone. We could have called the police, and maybe Ellen would have if I weren't there, but when she threatened to pick up the phone I gave her a pleading look, and she desisted. I wanted to defuse the situation without costing Robertson the presidency, and I knew that a call to the police would mean the end of all such hopes. I wasn't any happier than Ellen was about what he was doing to the apartment, which we had just cleaned the day before, but I also couldn't see giving him over to the media, which I knew would jump on this story like a flock of vultures. I mean, could anyone really blame the guy for cracking under the enormous strain of a presidential campaign that had been going on now for practically a year? Instead of taking drastic action, I tried to reason with the man.

"Robertson, don't worry," I said, galloping into the living room. "The kitty will turn up somewhere. No need to tear the place apart."

"I've got to find her. She's allergic to certain nuts and berries. Anything could happen."

"I'll help you look. Could you put that television down?"

"She belonged to my Aunt, who never made it far in the space program."

"For God's sake man, pull yourself together. Let's talk it out. I can help you get through this. But first you've got to put down the 36-inch television set. And also would you please get down off that 10-foot ladder?"

"I made cookies, and they were chocolaty!"

I suppose I should have known then that things were not going to work out for the best. When the cat finally revealed herself at the foot of the ladder, shooting out from underneath the china cabinet and scampering across the floor toward the overstuffed eggplant-colored Pottery Barn loveseat, Robertson threw his hands up in celebration of the proof of her continued existence, the upward and outward movement of such throwing being enough to cause the television, a birthday gift just received from Ellen's stockbroker ex-husband but a week ago, to plummet out of Robertson's plump hands directly down upon my prize winning (3rd at the 2002 Midwest Championship; 2nd at the 2003 Nationals) Japanese Fir, which, needless to say, will not be winning another prize any time soon. Robertson too nearly tumbled off the ladder, but with the grace of a six-time all-star left winger he was able to right himself on the second highest rung, where he took a seat and looked down dumbfoundedly upon the chaos below.

As wisps of smoke slipped from the television's broken casing and fir sap dripped upon the newly washed pine floor, the soft squeaking of the tiny white kitten under the loveseat could barely be heard over my wife's heavy sobs and Robertson's incoherent mumblings. "I am like the wind," he muttered. "Feel me blow."

Though I knew it would probably mean the end of my political career, I felt no choice at this point but to ask the candidate to leave.

The Joy of Shopping For Odds and Ends

Otto and Mortimer, their slate grey morning coats fluttering in the brisk November wind, inflate kickballs for the upcoming match. I am on the monkey bars, eyeing the heavens and contemplating the nation's sickness. On the well-worn pages of a small notebook, I catalog the infirmities, make detailed lists of the pros and cons, plot strategies for solving the problems of our ailing homeland. The playground is on edge waiting for Nerwood Spillipong's next move, but I keep focused on the task at hand. If I let my guard down now, I may never understand what is truly behind all this.

You approach the monkey bars, demand we retire to the seesaw to review the Fantasy Scrabble standings, and I comply. Who am I to resist your argyle skirt, that fancy angora sweater purchased just last week at Chess King, those pink and white ribbons in your hair dyed turquoise?

Together we examine the Scrabble Reports, printed freshly off the internet. I am crestfallen. Edley, that dope! How could he have missed such an obvious Bingo? Now my chances of winning the Grand Prize have plunged to nearly nil, and the possibility of traveling to the Algarve for Easter has fallen hopelessly out of reach. Why did I ever decide to draft his inconsistent ass in the first round anyway?

Mortimer skips towards us, bounces the largest kickball off the top of my head. Game time!

It is girls against boys, the annual Friday the 13th tradition, so you and I let our hands slip slowly apart, join our respective teams. I am watching the bounce of your skirt when Spillipong approaches, tugging Mrs. Whiteside by the wrist. "There they are," he screams, "acting in derogation of duty, placing their own interests above those of the collective." Whiteside is overwhelmed by Spillipong's attention to detail, unwavering uprightness that reminds her of Reagan, Jesse Jackson, Chiang Kai Shek. This is what I had expected, so I am not taken by surprise. Otto is, however, and he faints, cracking his head on the blacktop.

Spillipong reacts by jumping up and down like a toddler, screeching and perhaps wetting the Jedi Knight robe he hasn't taken off since Halloween. "They're in derogation of duty!" he blubbers, "they undermined the interests of the group for their own benefit!" Whiteside grabs my lapel and drags me to the Room of Heat, promises Spillipong a permanent appointment to the Student Council, inexplicably praises Derrida to the heavens.

In transit, I wonder what my cross-Atlantic pen-pal Loriana looks like. Do her eyes resemble sapphires? Are her thighs thicker, sweeter, more voluptuous than yours? I guess now I'll never now. Damn that crazy Edley and his neo-futuristic Falun Gong inspired bullshit!

Six hours pass in the hot box before I am let off with a warning and a firm pat on the rump, a short speech about the importance of virtue, social mores, cooking with salt substitutes. I've missed the game; in my absence, the boys lose 14-12 on a late frame homer by Melba Sandoval, who has recently been spied necking feverishly with Nerwood Spillipong behind the nearside dumpsters after track practice.

Following a quick trip to the infirmary to visit the slowly recovering and insanely muttering Otto, Mortimer and I seek some solace at the local Target. While I peruse the aisles for knick knacks and gewgaws, Morty browses the baby supplies aisle, as he fears, not without some substantial basis, that he has impregnated his second cousin playing strip Twister at Otto's Bar Mitzvah party the Sunday before last. I think of the possibility of bringing a baby into the world with you some day and frankly I have my doubts. Your beauty overwhelms me, it does, but I am young, and our nation is in peril. Is this really a place to raise a child, I'm not so sure. Luckily, I lose myself for precious moments in these endless aisles, with their placemats and small trash cans and cleaning supplies and picture frames and electric toothbrushes. I reach a sort of pleasant repose, but then find myself in the stationary aisle where I suddenly remember all the difficulties. I place several small notebooks into my basket and make my way slowly to the cashiers.

Henry Clay Will Solve Our Problems

*A*pril *2009. At a Qdoba in downtown Winnetka, a mother and daughter discuss the latter's college plans. Nearby sits an older distinguished gentleman wearing exclusively American-made clothing. This is Henry Clay.*

Mother: I don't understand why Northwestern isn't good enough. They've got a great chemistry department.

Daughter: [visibly annoyed] Geez, Mom, how many times do I have to tell you this? Dalhousie's chemistry department is totally awesome. It's like the best university in the Maritimes, for god's sake. Plus, I'm sick of Chicago. I need to expand my horizons. I want to study overseas. Ugh.

Henry Clay leans over to speak with the two ladies.

Henry Clay: Excuse me. I was sitting here enjoying my Signature Ancho Chile Barbecue Burrito, and I couldn't help but overhear you discussing college plans. Why doesn't the young lady give Northwestern a try for one year. If she still doesn't like it, she can transfer to Dalhousie.

Mother and Daughter look at each other. Both of them seem to think Mr. Clay's idea makes for a nice compromise. They voice their assent.

Henry Clay: Ahhh, good.

Henry Clay grins devilishly, like he did after orchestrating his successful (kind of) resolution to the Nullification Crisis of 1833.

December 2010. In Mexico City, a U.S. climate change negotiator argues with his Chinese counterpart.

Chinese Negotiator: We absolutely cannot accept this proposal. The developed world has created this global warming crisis, and you must lead us out of it. The United States must pledge to cut emissions by 50% and provide low-cost technology to developing nations.

U.S. Negotiator: My country will never agree to such drastic cuts unless yours agrees to the same. China is the greatest emitter of greenhouse gases in the entire world.

A dapper man enters and takes a seat next to the two negotiators.

Henry Clay: [with booming voice, somewhat out of place in the small conference room] Gentlemen, surely we can find some compromise!

Chinese Negotiator: I'm a woman.

Henry Clay: And I am Henry Clay, the Great Compromiser. I have an idea that will appeal to both of your great nations. Neither of you want to decrease emissions unless the other one decreases emissions, right? So why don't you both not decrease emissions?

A pause.

U.S. Negotiator: I'm cool with that. You?

Chinese Negotiator: Umm, it seems wrong, but....

Henry Clay: Then it's settled!

Another pause.

Henry Clay: Did I mention that I invented the mint julep?

April 2011. In a bar outside Fenway Park in Boston, a Boston Red Sox fan argues with a New York Yankee fan about which baseball club is superior.

Yankee Fan: You suck.

Red Sox Fan: You wicked suck.

Henry Clay: Why, good evening, fellows. I see that you two cannot agree regarding which baseball club is superior. May I suggest that you agree to root for a different team that you both enjoy? Perhaps the Kansas City Athletics?

The two fans stare at Henry Clay, then back at each other, then back at Henry Clay. This goes on for maybe thirty seconds. Things become uncomfortable.

Henry Clay: Or you could fight a duel. I did that twice.

May 2011: The daughter who wanted to attend Dalhousie University but didn't because of Henry Clay's compromise proposal and instead ended up never leaving her parents' house dines on greasy pork chops while her disgusted mother looks on.

Mother: Are you ever going to move out of the basement?

Daughter: [mouth full of food] I don't know. No. [burps]

Mother: Damn that Henry Clay.

Henry Clay pops into the kitchen, still wearing all American fabrics, including Lee brand dungarees.

Mother: Oh, great. Look who it is.

Daughter: I'm not going back to college. Ever.

Mother: [to Henry Clay] You got any more great ideas, hotshot?

March 2012: In downtown Seattle, a man and a woman debate which fast food outlet to visit for lunch.

Man: Let's go to Burger King. They flame broil.

Woman: But Wendy's is so much better. They have square patties.

Henry Clay: [tapping woman on shoulder] Maybe you should consider an alternative. Instead of having a burger this afternoon, maybe you should go to Qdoba. I hear they have a terrific signature Ancho Chile Barbecue Burrito for only $4.95.

Man: Oh, look, it's Henry Clay, here to push one of his famous "compromises" on us.

Woman: [brushing Henry Clay's hand off her shoulder] Yeah, what's in it for you, Clay? I bet you get a kickback for each signature Ancho Chile Barbecue Burrito you convince someone to buy. That's right, isn't it?

Man: What a corrupt bargain!

Henry Clay: I'll fucking kill you.

Croquet, Okay

Beth kneels on the warm grass, squints through one eye, decides the angle is all off. She won't be able to pound her grapefruit-sized red ridged ball through the weirdly angled wicket in only one shot. It will take two. One to get the ball close, and one to punch it through. She's not likely to get the chance, though, as Evan's big blue ball isn't far away, and he's got the next turn. There's a good possibility she'll have to take her next shot from under the porch, or in the midst of bushes, or, if Evan is feeling particularly nefarious and can pull it off, from the bottom of the driveway or the other side of the street.

This is backyard croquet. They've been playing it all summer, drunken afternoons under the inviting California sun, barbecue grill flared up, the smell of tangy smoked chicken in the air, Guns N' Roses and XTC blaring on the stereo. Evan licks his lips in anticipation of sending Beth far away in search of her ball. Josh and Sarah stand nearby, gossiping about various professors. They've finished three years of a Ph.D., but at least three more lie ahead. Ted, Beth's odd little boyfriend, sits in a lawn chair by the back door sipping a Sierra Nevada and watching the action. His chair is within the boundaries of the croquet court, but then again what isn't? The rest of the group can't quite figure out why Beth is with Ted. He is quiet and not easily classifiable. Beth is devoted, though, so questions about their relationship remain muted, not openly vented. The last of the group—Matt and Laura—are inside cutting vegetables, marinating meat. They are a couple, engaged just last month, and they will play in the next match. Unlike the others, they are not pursuing higher degrees in science. Laura teaches high school, Matt studies law. Matt and Evan are friends from way back, from the college summer they kicked in headlights, made stir-fries from compact discs.

Beth stands next to the ball and clunks it with the mallet, golf swing style. In the backyard, croquet players do not swing their mallets between their legs. Thudded solidly, the ball rolls across the yard, over some loose stones, down a slight ditch and then up again, through a patch of small twigs, coming to a rest about a foot from the wicket. With another turn, she could easily poke it through, but she doesn't have another turn, and Evan grins devilishly as he strides toward his blue ball, his mallet swinging confidently at his side.

Evan puts his beer bottle on the ground next to him and sizes up the situation. If he wanted to, he could simply pop his blue ball right through the wicket and start his advance upon the next wicket—the one under the lip of the porch, next to the bush with all the thistles. But that wouldn't be prudent. Beth could hit him on her next turn and knock him out of the yard, which is something Evan can't afford right now because Josh is already two wickets ahead and Sarah is approaching quickly. Plus, it wouldn't be much fun. Far better to send Beth flying. Evan gives his ball a tap, and it clunks against Beth's. Now Evan has to concentrate. He places his ball right next to Beth's, clamps his left foot down on it, and prepares to give Beth's ball a long ride into croquet oblivion.

"Excuse me," Evan says in an artificially deep voice to Josh and Sarah, still enraptured in their conversation about professors. They are standing directly between Beth's ball and the side of the yard that leads to the driveway and street. "Please move."

"Tee, hee, hee," Ted twitters from his seated perch at the other side of the yard.

Evan turns and looks at Ted for a moment. He wonders: *Who is this little man?* Josh and Sarah move out of the way without objection. Had they not been in such deep conversation regarding the rumors of Professor Harry Feller's possible sex-change operation they might have issued a caustic retort, but the discussion is too important to put on hold. Beth covers her eyes with her right hand and peeks out between fingers at Evan, now deeply concentrating on hitting his ball cleanly. The sound of Matt and Laura chopping celery can be heard, ever slightly, over Josh and Sarah's chattering.

Evan takes several practice swings, lifting up his mallet to shoulder height and beyond, then bringing it down at half-speed to where his ball sits on the ground. This could be really bad, Beth thinks. As bad as the time Matt hit Ted's ball so hard that Ted had to get on his bike to chase it down the street. As bad as anything backyard croquet has ever seen.

Taking a deep breath, Evan takes his backswing for real this time. He pauses for a split second at the top, then whips the mallet down like Tiger Woods off the tee at Pebble Beach. The mallet makes solid contact, fierce contact, but it is with Evan's left foot, not the ball. He lets out a scream, plummets to the toasty grass. Beth lets out a celebratory yelp. She's happy about the miscue, not yet worried about her friend's metatarsal bones. Josh and Sarah pause from their discussion and look with some concern at their friend, who is writhing in both pain and embarrassment on the yard's floor. Ted chirps out his usual "tee hee hee." Hearing the ruckus, Laura calls out through the open kitchen window to find out what happened. Beth yells back: "Evan hit his foot. Evan hit his foot."

"Fucking dope!" Matt barks.

Maybe ten minutes pass before play resumes. Evan walks off the injury the best he can. He is still limping, but the pain eventually subsides. Though he continues to play in the croquet match, he never really recovers from the foot-smashing incident. Beth, however, spirits lifted by her new found croquet life, plays the rest of the game like someone who has walked away from a fiery car crash. She takes each shot as though it might be her last. Repeatedly she utters the phrase: *Seize the Turn*. She overcomes Josh and sends his ball into a ditch. Josh becomes dispirited and can't get himself back in the game. Sarah makes a bit of a run for it at the end, but there's no catching Beth, and when Beth's ball becomes the first to make it all the way around and hit the center peg, the mallet that she throws in the air to celebrate the victory comes only a hair away from thumping Evan on the head as it twirls its way back down to the earth.

* * *

Real croquet, it turns out, differs sharply from the backyard version. They find this out on a Saturday outing at the San Francisco Croquet Club. Evan reads in the Chronicle that the Club is seeking new members for its competitive league, and so on a bright lovely Bay Area morning the seven friends pile into two Honda Civics and make their way up the Peninsula to the City to try their hand at real croquet, on a real croquet lawn. How hard could it be, they figure? How hard could it be for a group of healthy, well-practiced youngsters to excel at a sport generally populated by effete, arthritic antiquarians?

They arrive full of vigor and hope, piling out of the two cars in front of a stately mansion near the top of one of San Francisco's magnificent hills. Looking out on the long swaths of grass to each side of the club's main building, thoughts turn to the upcoming San Francisco Open. They all agree that one of them will win the tournament, but they cannot agree on who, specifically, will prevail. Beth has been playing well lately it is true, but Evan has been the most consistent player over the summer's long course, and Matt's dead-on accuracy has to put him within the top three at least, even if he often lacks the attention span to see through any particular game to victory. Ted, most agree, will not win the Open.

A distinguished gentleman who introduces himself as Edward Wharton, outfitted entirely in crisp white, greets them upon arrival. "Welcome to the Club," he says. "It is always nice when we find youngsters who are interested in the sport. It bodes well for our future." He leads the group to a side lawn where two elderly patrons, also dressed completely in white, are practicing their shots. The old woman, her name is Hilda, encourages her geriatric husband Gerald, in his attempt to tap his red ball through a perfectly placed wicket four feet away. "You can do it, Gerald," she says, and she is right. Gerald hits the ball squarely, and it glides smoothly over the finely trimmed grass directly through the center of the wicket. "Oh, goodie!" Hilda claps.

It is clear that they are no longer in the backyard. The perfection of the lawn is what they all notice first. No bramble bushes here, no garden hoses or ant hills to traverse, no rotted wooden boards with rusted nails sticking out to avoid. Everything else is flawless too, from the tall solid mallets to the straight square wickets to the gleaming balls, unscratched by pavement or tiny pointed pebbles, so unlike their own shabby equipment. They look down at their inapt clothing, mismatched colors, blue jeans clashing with orange t-shirts, slogans like "I Always Get My Drugs at Moe's," so apparently witty back home, now seem blatantly out-of-place. Evan thinks to look around for signs of casual alcohol consumption, but he finds no evidence of any beer, not even an empty plastic cup that might have recently held a gin-and-tonic. He thinks: *Oh, dear lord, what have we done?*

Edward suggests that two members of the group compete against Gerald and Hilda in an exhibition match. Everyone else will watch and learn the rules peculiar to regulation play. At one point, Sarah mentions to Edward that the group has been playing backyard croquet all summer. Edward grins and nods his head ever so slightly. "Yes, dear, I'm sure you have."

Hilda goes first. She stands next to the ball and clunks it with the mallet, between-the-legs style. On the lawn, croquet players do not swing their mallets as though they were golf clubs. This slight deviation places Evan and Beth at a bit of a disadvantage. Beth's first swing completely misses the ball. This is almost physically impossible, but the do-over swing, generously allowed by Gerald, nearly does the same; the ball ricochets off Beth's right ankle and bounces backward. Not a good start. Evan's ball, unlike Beth's, goes forward, but much too quickly. The black ball just about sails over the other edge of the lawn, but luckily it bounces off the side of the far wicket and comes to a rest about 30 yards in the wrong direction. Meanwhile, Gerald and Hilda effortlessly glide through the first few wickets. Though their combined ages exceed those of Evan and Beth's by almost a hundred years, Gerald and Hilda are well on their way to winning the exhibition game.

Before long, though, Evan and Beth, urged on by the cheering of the others and Edward's patient instructions, begin to get the hang of the between-the-legs swing, and they make their way back into semi-respectable contention. At one point, Evan aims for Hilda's ball from ten yards away and hits it dead on. "Nice roquet!" Edward exclaims, as Evan strides forward to send Hilda's ball into croquet oblivion.

Ever since the foot-smashing incident in the backyard, Evan has been careful about this kind of shot, the shot that Edward refers to as the "croquet stroke," much to everyone's delight. This time he won't miss, he won't bruise any toes, won't end up face first on the well-coiffed lawn. He looks out beyond the lawn's edge. There is a steep hill that rolls down to a line of blossoming shrubs. He thinks that with enough topspin he could maybe reach them. The thought of watching the octogenarian hobble down the hill with her cane and scavenge through the shrubs for her green ball makes Evan smile wickedly in anticipation. He places his ball next to hers and steps on it solidly. Before anyone can stop him, Evan swings the mallet like Greg Norman off the tee at Augusta and slams it into his ball. Hilda's ball soars off the lawn, just like Evan imagined, and bounces with such velocity that it is still rolling when it hits the line of shrubs and disappears.

"Oh, goodness!" squeals Hilda, grasping her chest.

"Sweet Jesus!" yelps Gerald.

"Tee hee hee," squawks Ted.

"What are you doing?" Edward demands, his voice raised, stomping briskly toward Evan, who is thrusting his mallet sky high in celebration of his perfect croquet stroke. "You can't do that here! What do you think this is, the suburbs? You can't put your foot on your ball when you hit the croquet stroke. You can't send someone out of bounds. Now, you'll have to go down and get the ball and bring it back up here."

Evan is crestfallen. He stops singing "We are the Champions" and looks at Edward in disbelief. "What? Are you kidding? You can't slam someone? What's the point?"

"I am not kidding. You must go retrieve that ball. I think you might have given poor Hilda a coronary."

"Aww," moans Evan. He throws the mallet down and goes off to retrieve the ball. Continuously he mutters: *What's the fucking point?* It takes him several minutes to find the ball in the shrubs and extract it from its tightly ensconced position between two limbs. When he finally makes it back up to the lawn, he finds Hilda sitting in a lawn chair. Gerald is fanning her with a copy of *The Atlantic Monthly*. Edward hands Hilda a glass of freshly squeezed orange juice, which she sips slowly. Evan meets up with the rest of the group. Collectively they wonder whether Hilda will return to the game and, if she does, whether she might be so frazzled by the incident that Evan and Beth could actually win this thing.

No such luck. After finishing her orange juice, Hilda shuffles back to the lawn, and they resume play. Evan and Beth make a few good shots, but the team is inconsistent and cannot keep up. Hilda and Gerald are toying with them. The two grandparents-many-times-over are thinking several moves ahead at all times. The game, as they say over and over, is like "chess on grass," a phrase that sends the twenty-somethings into a mild state of depression each time they hear it. Gerald makes it all the way around the course and back again to the very last wicket before either Evan or Beth can make it to that wicket for even the first time. He has lapped them. When Gerald hits the center peg, there seems no sense in playing the rest of the game to see who comes in second, since Hilda is only two wickets away herself.

* * *

Back home on the Peninsula, the group sits around the living room eating reheated leftovers, microwaved TV dinners. Nobody says much. They have been humiliated by the day. None of them will ever return to the San Francisco Croquet club. The backyard croquet set, too, will fall into disuse. Breaking the silence, Ted tells a story about how his mother refused to buy him a pet rabbit when he was nine, but no one is interested. "What the hell are you talking about?" Evan blurts. Beth looks at Evan angrily. "It's okay, Ted," she says, putting an arm around Ted's shoulder. "It will all be okay."

Eenie Meenie

Eenie Meenie

O ver a shared plate of calamari and glasses of Barbaresco, Dan and Hannah discuss the details of their proposed affair. They are both attorneys, mid-level associates at the same large downtown firm, so they are quite familiar with the task of negotiating specifics. Dan asks about the location of their trysts; would they happen at a hotel, and if so, one in town or a suburban location? Hannah wonders about the affair's length and how it might end. She asks Dan whether the affair would be unilaterally terminable without prior notice or instead if some sort of hearing, e.g., an opportunity to respond to the terminator's proposed reasons for termination, would be appropriate. Dan shakes his head and pours more wine. A hearing, of course, he says. Even cheaters have their rights. Hannah is lovely in the dim candlelight of this romantic restaurant that he cannot even imagine visiting with his wife of ten years. Hannah's scent reminds him of high school. Not his own high school, perhaps, but the high school of the nation's collective imagination, something one might find expressed in a song by John Cougar, or a nostalgic television show featuring bright pastel colors, or something of the sort.

Miney Moe

Back at home that night, Dan explains to his wife Maria that he has been working late on merger documents and regrets his tardy return. Maria may or may not have noticed his absence, but she gives him a peck on the cheek before asking him to take out the trash.

Garbage brought to the curb, Dan strolls past Maria, who is sipping something clear over ice and cackling on the phone with her odious mother, and pokes his head into his son's bedroom. There he is, only four, wrapped up in pajamas featuring some second-tier superhero, his face planted so deep into a striped pillow Dan wonders if Andrew can even breathe. Dan thinks back to when Andrew was just home from the hospital, unable even to turn over on his own, sometimes sleeping sitting up in his car seat next to their bed, Dan waking to even the smallest movement, the slightest moan or sound. He tiptoes to Andrew's bed, softly touches his son's feathery hair with outstretched fingertips. Dan's heart flutters. This, he figures, is not something he can do without.

Catch a Tiger

They are in the office together, it is late, and there is a crunch. A response to something or other is due in the morning, so authorities must be assembled, paragraphs drafted. The partner in charge is in Kansas issuing invectives left and right on a separate matter, so the filing is left in the hands of Dan and Hannah. The two work furiously, keying sophisticated searches into expensive databases and ordering spicy Thai noodles from the local Bangkok Express. At one o'clock, Dan finally loosens his tie. He is reading a draft of the document's penultimate section when Hannah barges into his office, throws the conclusion down in front of him, settles into the leather chair on the far side of Dan's desk. He looks up and realizes that Hannah is bare-legged; her opaque stockings, once pulled tautly over slender calves, have been discarded. The realization just about overwhelms him. At this point only his exhaustion (and perhaps the seventeen inch computer monitor between them) keeps him from leaping over the desk into Hannah's lap.

By the Toe

At dinner with Maria's sister and her husband, Dan orders a second sidecar when the talk turns to Glenn Close. "Creepy," says Maria, chewing on a maraschino cherry from a quickly slurped whiskey sour. "Ghoulish," adds her sister Tammy, who pulls her aquamarine silk shirt back over an exposed pink bra strap. The ladies volunteer their favorite Close movies. One mentions *The Big Chill*, the other *Dangerous Liaisons*. But those are not the films Dan is thinking of, and he's never really been much of a fan in any event.

If He Hollers

Later that night, Dan drives the babysitter home, pops alkali tablets, realizes he no longer recognizes himself. The fact that every middle-aged man in the history of the universe (save perhaps Trump, a few other idiots) has eventually realized the same thing brings little comfort. Out he goes to the living room. Despite the late hour and her drunken state, Maria sits at the dining room table staring at an Excel spreadsheet on her laptop. She is entering figures, groaning, recalculating. Dan knows that she wants to build a pool in the backyard with a swim-up bar and is trying to make it happen by manipulating financial accounts, mortgaging the family's future, hypothesizing nonexistent sources of wealth. One column, to Dan's great dismay, is entitled "Potential Craps Winnings." He approaches her from the back, drapes his arms around her shoulders, smooches her bare neck. "Have you figured it out yet?" he asks. "I've almost got it," she answers. "What are the odds on a hard six again?" He buries his nose deep in her thick curls, asks her to come to bed. She shakes him off, insists on finishing the present calculations. When he sighs in defeat, she stops what she's doing, turns full circle, takes hold of his hand, gives it a soft kiss. He smiles, but then she turns back to the computer, resumes her analysis. His wife, Dan knows all too well, doles out her affection in teaspoonfuls.

Let Him Go

Their boss is back from the Midwest, and he's fucking pissed at Dan and Hannah. In his office, the two potential lovers slouch in leather chairs and absorb the scolding like schoolchildren. The document they worked on all night is not up to snuff, not even close to what is expected from lawyers of their caliber. The partner yells at them for forgetting important legal authorities, misphrasing critical arguments, violating grammar rules "that any mildly retarded six year old could follow." When he's not screaming or burying his face in his oversized hands, the partner shakes the flawed document at Dan and Hannah like each is half of a two headed puppy that has just soiled an expensive handmade carpet. They both apologize, but that doesn't seem to do the trick. The main problem is in the second to last section, the one entitled "The Bank Holding Act of 1948 Provides Few, if any, Restraints on Credit Reporting Corporations Under the Restatement (Third's) Principle of Restorative Justice, and Whatnot." "But the Bank Holding Act wasn't promulgated until 1954!" blurts the partner. "And Restatement Third of *what*?" Dan knows that he is responsible for these particular blunders, but he is still surprised when he hears Hannah volunteer this information to their boss. "That was Dan's section of the document," she says. The boss turns his fiery gaze in Dan's direction, and Dan in turn spins and stares at Hannah. *What the hell is the matter with you*, his eyes ask, but her attention is focused on a complicated paperweight that holds down her boss's bonus recommendations, due in the managing partner's office by Tuesday COB.

Out Goes Y-O....

A fortnight later, differences behind them, Dan and Hannah sit at a hotel bar in suburban Indianapolis, downing classic American lagers one after the other to celebrate their hard fought victory. Apparently the judge ignored the minor mistakes, saw through to the merits of the summary judgment motion. Back on the West Coast, Andrew misses his dad, now out of town for nearly a week. The boy begs his mom to let him call Dan, but Maria is upset that Andrew hasn't finished his entire serving of broccoli. When a tear drips down Andrew's cheek, Maria finally relents and makes him a deal: if he finishes every last piece of broccoli, he can call his father. Andrew isn't entirely happy with the proposal but figures he doesn't have much choice. His mom does not generally renegotiate. Maria retires to the living room to watch the local news and play a little solitaire. After she leaves, Andrew stares hopelessly at his plate. He pops a stalk into his mouth and chews. And chews and chews and chews. It takes him maybe three minutes to finish the entire floret; since there are ten left and he needs a three minute break between each one, it takes him about an hour to finish the plateful. The sour taste remains in his throat, countless grassy stubs stick stubbornly between his tiny teeth. As soon as the last piece is gone, though, he yells eagerly to his mom, who says she'll be in to place the call just as soon as her game is done.

At that very moment, Dan and Hannah, having settled up with the barkeep for the nine beers they just finished, step into the elevator that will take them to their rooms on the fourth floor. A Muzak version of Purple Haze plays too loudly in the tiny space. Even though it is late on a winter night and they've been smoking, Dan finds Hannah's scent enthralling. She smells like autumn, the Homecoming dance, a crisp Thanksgiving morning football game against the cross-town rivals. He has no idea what he's doing, or what he plans to do.

When they alight from the elevator, there is an awkward moment or two before they decide to go together to Dan's room. There, he has a bottle of scotch they will use for a nightcap. Dan has trouble opening the door with his keycard that in his nervous drunken state he keeps inserting in the wrong direction. Hannah giggles, touches Dan's arm tenderly, shows him the correct method of insertion. The light turns green at the same time that Andrew screams for his mother to hurry up and call his dad in Indiana. Maria tells him she'll be right there, that her game is almost over. She flips the cards, one two three, looking for something that will help her get the last ace out, free up the five of clubs. Flip, flip, flip. At the table, Andrew sighs, then pours himself another tall glass of water. Though time is the only cure for the nasty taste that lingers on his tongue, he drinks the water down quickly, in one gulp, hoping that maybe, just maybe, it will wash the bitterness away.

Eyes Like Kumquats, Lips Like a Cocked Gun

The computer is humming, but Gerson cannot hear it above the clanking and clinking of the antiquated ventilation system purportedly designed to provide some sort of air conditioning relief to his steamy office. He looks at the proposed legislation in front of him, then the screen. The bill, the screen. A dropped glance at the sheaf of cases he thinks may have the answer to the constitutional quandary. Back to the bill. Then the screen. The bill, the sheaf of cases, the screen. The office is very, very hot. It is twelve o'clock. Gerson breaks for lunch.

In the lunchroom, a group of young attorneys, his colleagues, shod in various shades of grey or blue wool, are discussing the reality television show from last night. Not having seen the show, Gerson has nothing to contribute, but he listens intently.

You speak to me, and it is like geraniums.

Morphology, Radge says, is the study of shapes, but I can't be sure he is telling the truth, for he oft dissembles. The kitchen is stuffy. I spin my head at the sound of a slamming refrigerator door, but all I see is trains. Locomotives, those things at the end, what are they called, cabooses? I guess it is true what you often told me. I live in a land they call "the Epilogue."

Gerson munches his sandwich, it is deviled ham. The colleagues discuss theories, suppositions. He takes a sip of lemonade. It is tart, but yet sweet, and he cannot participate.

Forget the Constitution. This is the real quandary.

It has been six, perhaps seven years since I have laid eyes on you, and now you have something to offer, it would seem. A consulting deal, a trilateral barometric something or other, I don't know what the hell you are talking about. You have on a red wool suit, who would have chosen such a thing? The papers you hand me are inscrutable. I look through them in search of some paragraph, some sentence, some phrase I can hold on to, but it is in vain. You shake your head. I don't know.

Gerson stands and looks out the window upon Pennsylvania Avenue. The tourists are flocking to the FBI building, but there are no tours there anymore. In the background, one colleague says something about the Falkland war to another. The second colleague compares the conflict to others that have come since, and a few that predated it. There is some discussion of the art of analogy, but Gerson can't focus on it. Outside, on the sidewalk, a man wearing tattered rags appears to be speaking to a squirrel. It is unclear whether the rodent responds, and if it doesn't, whether this is because it lacks the capability or the will.

When Radge returned from the South Pacific, he had stories to tell and knickknacks to distribute. Mine was a magnet, there was a slogan. Once again I glance at the door of the electric rectangular cooling device but see only automated transport units. The magnet has disappeared, it could be under the pillow. I am not allowed near the pillow anymore, though, because I will not fully shower. There are rules, this is one of them. I run my hand over the smooth metal and turn to look at you. Is there a field of daffodils nearby, or is it simply "happening" again?

Gerson has had his fill, and he returns to the office. The work that has drawn him to the District has become unwieldy; it no longer makes any sense. He too thinks of Radge and the trinket from the islands that was lost soon thereafter. Gerson has always dreamed of visiting Fiji, but the scandal has put his dreams on hold. This Radge, this friend of ours, his campaign has hit the headlines, but somehow he cannot evade the Fourth Estate's insistent questioning. They have discovered certain transactions involving diamonds that went on long ago, under cover of night, in the shadows of ivy draped classroom buildings. You will not come clean regarding these gems, and so we all suffer.

You with your face, it has wiped us out. We will all land in the grave soon because of it.

Embedded

At the dining room table, I shovel mashed potatoes into my mouth, try to get the son to talk about his afternoon soccer game. My next report is coming up soon, so there's no time to dilly-dally. I turn my full attention to the muddy teenage boy. "So," I inquire, "did you register any goals or assists in your four to two triumph over the cross-town rivals this afternoon?"

The son looks at me like I'm a bag of horseshit dropped off with the afternoon newspaper. He picks up a dinner roll and flings it. "Think quick," he says, right before the roll ricochets off my forehead and lands in the salad bowl.

"Sam!" exclaims the mother, "don't throw bread at the journalist." The little girl on the other side of the table—her name is Tanya—laughs excitedly, though it's not clear whether she's laughing because Sam threw the roll or because her mother yelled at Sam.

Fuck it, I think, I don't need this crap. I've got other ways to find out about the JV soccer game. I leave the table, take the roll with me, scowl at all involved.

Next to the jungle gym in the playground behind the junior high school, I pass out smokes to a substantial subset of the cheerleading squad, court the good graces of the barely pubescent class of 2009. As the kids light up with a book of matches I took from a favorite casino before my family staged its intervention, I click on the portable machine and tell them they're on the record. The tall one with the full lips and the retro bangs doesn't like this one bit and tells me to talk to the hand, which is weird because she isn't even holding up one of her hands.

The rest of them, though, are eager to speak. I drill them on the facts, confirm every detail with at least two sources. After much playground talk and the trading of questionable inside jokes, consensus is reached on the notion that the kid scored one goal in the first half and received a yellow card for calling the opposing goalie some sort of unfavorable appellation regarding cheese in the second. Less certainty, however, surrounds the suggestion raised by the perky brunette captain with the oversized thermos that Sam also assisted on Yepperson's game clinching header in the final minute.

On this latter point, the petite strawberry blonde who resembles some sort of twisted red panda staunchly insists that she saw DeLuca, and not our hero, set up Hatfield's set up of Yepperson's brilliant bop that every junior high kid in town will be talking about until at least the middle of next week. The two or three members of the group who are not currently texting each other issue virulent rebukes of the redhead's position, but I lack both the time and the will to resolve the discrepancy. I'll have to employ generally accepted practices to handle the ambiguity, but that's nothing new for me. I did it countless times reporting for the Network before the incident.

Ten minutes before show time. I pass out the rest of the sizzle sticks and head for home.

I deliver the report smoothly, convey the necessary information, provide insightful commentary. As always I am nervous up until the moment we go live; the fact that I'm under the glare of a mechanized web-cam and not a traditional human-wielded video camera makes no difference. I am meticulous, lay out every important event relating to the Winston family that has transpired since the lunchtime report. Dinner is recounted in detail: the mushiness of the chicken tenders, the bitter arugula salad, the roll-throwing episode and Tanya's subsequent giggling; even my angry recusal and associated scowl receive oblique mention. An entire section of the webcast is devoted to after school activities: Tanya's finger-painting play date at little Sally Silverstone's gets a full five minutes of coverage, including a critical segment on the quality of the resulting work (it sucks, even for a four year old, but I exercise discretion and refer to the piece falsely as "mildly promising"), and of course the soccer game occupies a prominent position. As to the issue of the assist on Yepperson's header, I say only that sources close to the incident differ regarding the exact nature of Samuel's contribution. At the end of the transmission, I conclude with a short editorial commentary in which I advocate (plead, really) for a softer, plusher style of toilet paper to be installed in the bathrooms, or at least in the bathroom down on my sad, lonely end of the upstairs hall.

Six hours later, after wrapping up the final report of the day, I lie quietly on my rented bed, stare vacantly at the ceiling. In another hour or two I will make my rounds of the house, check that everything is in order, assure myself there's no need to break the boss's concentration for a special after hours broadcast. In the meantime, I listen for any hallway movements worth investigating and hear nothing, drift into the comfortable zone of near sleep. Here I have returned to the casino of choice, the true land of a thousand points of light, the cling clang clanging of the slot machines like a jazz starlet's husky voice to these sordid ears. So what if it is Easter morning, the same set of characters from the night before surround the table, that old guy with the pants hiked up to his nipples, drinking something dark and betting sporadically on long shots that come in only often enough to keep his night alive. I am rolling the dice, the point is nine, cigarette smoking in my other hand, full odds behind the pass line, pressed the four and ten, two on the yo, I'll take five on the hard six, dealer, better bet the field while I'm at it. The dice roll to the far side of the table, this way and that, but they don't seem to stop, just keep tumbling, tumbling, tumbling on pastures of green up to the horizon and beyond, beyond, beyond.

I wake at dawn, the dog licking my hand like some sort of fudgsicle. Blearily I realize where I am, that I've missed the mid-night walkthrough. That's probably okay; there's little chance anything much happened while I was in dreamland. The tot sleeps like a rock. Sam is still too cowardly to sneak out after bedtime looking for trouble. And Sheila, the wife, well, she hasn't left the house after nightfall in months.

I remove my hand from the retriever's slobbering mouth and rub my eyes with it. It's clear: Another shitty day lies ahead. This job's peculiar combination of stress and pointlessness is new to me, not something I ever had to deal with at the Network. If I wasn't getting paid so much, and if I hadn't been fired from my last place of employment for running a high stakes dice game in the alley outside Studio B, and if I didn't owe fifteen grand at twenty-one percent interest to a multi-national credit dispensing corporation, I wouldn't have even considered taking the position to begin with.

First report of the day isn't until noon, so I grab my notebook and trudge slowly down several flights of stairs to the kitchen. I enter, am immediately engulfed by the warm breath of pancakes and the nauseating sweet stench of syrup pooled on plates covered with half-eaten breakfasts. Unwashed glasses and mugs and silverware cover the table and every other horizontal surface in the room, as well as one or two of the slanted ones. Nobody is present; the meal is over, and the maid hasn't yet arrived to clean the aftermath. From the adjacent television room, the screeches and thunks of some idiotic newfangled video game roar over the twittering of the smallest child, who struggles in the foyer with a hula hoop three times too large for her tiny body. I take a cup emblazoned with the name of my boss's firm from the cupboard and pour myself a cup of thick coffee that was probably prepared hours ago. It is bitter, and it is sandy, and I drink the whole cup before venturing a single step outside the kitchen.

I am looking for Sheila, want to ask her some questions about her burgeoning mid-day yoga practice for my upcoming special report, but I don't see her anywhere. I make my way to the foyer and take a knee so I can address the little one at eye level. "Hi ya," I say. "How's your hula hoop doing?" "It stinks, will you play with me?" she answers. I've never had kids of my own, and never much liked other peoples' kids, but this one's all right. She's cute and funny and strangely sophisticated in a way that makes her seem more mature than anyone else in the house. Add to that the pity I feel because her parents are never around and her brother is an annoying little shit, and I almost feel like spending the next hour playing hula hoops with the squirt. But if there's one thing we learned above all others at the Journalism Academy, it's to never become too emotionally involved with the objects of our investigation, always maintain objectivity, remain professionally aloof. I give her a smile and say "no thank you." She grimaces. I inquire regarding her mother's whereabouts. She points in the direction of the garage and mocks smoking a cigarette, blowing out the fake smoke like some trashy film noir harlot. I express gratitude, pinch her cheek, head off to the multi-Lexus-ensconcing garage.

The garage is thick with the smoke of expensive Egyptian cigarettes. Sheila sits on the trunk of the sedan, smoking and weeping. The floor below her is littered with butts, ashes, spent tissues. Usually, Sheila keeps her dyed blonde hair impeccably styled with gels and mousses imported from several Old World capitals, but today it is pulled back into a ponytail secured with a blue rubber band that might have held together the morning newspaper. My boss's faded Dartmouth sweatshirt hangs loosely on her small frame. She uncharacteristically wears no sapphire necklaces. I realize that I have come upon a unique and important event, one that may present my first real challenge, not to mention opportunity, of this odd assignment.

I take an uneasy step in Sheila's direction, but she is busy sobbing and doesn't notice me. With notebook in my right hand and pencil in my left, I approach further and cough conspicuously to get her attention. The mischievous ploy works. Sheila turns to face me, sucks up a clot of snot, bares her artificially whitened teeth. "What do you want?" she demands. "I see you are crying," I respond. "Oh, are you fucking Sherlock Holmes now?" she sputters. "Christiane Aman-fucking-pour or something?" "Can I get you anything?" I ask. "A tissue?" As her answer, she holds up a fistful of tissues and shakes it at me. "Look," I say. "I have a job to do. You know that. So I'll ask you this only once, and then I'll leave. Would you care to comment on the reason for your crying? You understand that I will have to report this. I only think it is fair to allow you a chance to explain." "Fuck off," she screams. "Get out of here." "Does that mean 'no comment'?" I ask. "No comment," she answers. "*No goddammned comment.*" I turn and go.

This is big. Big, big, BIG. Out of the garage I quickly contemplate my options. Report the new development at lunch? Investigate further, wait until I know more before springing the news? Neither course seems quite right. No, I must go live now, interrupt the day's goings on, deliver my first Special Report, give the story the import it deserves. I try to remember what the boss is up to today but can't recall. Taking a seat on the stairs heading up toward the main floor, I flip open the notebook, consult Saturday's schedule. Shit, he's in a deposition all morning. Defending no doubt the rights of industry captains against the frivolous claims of overzealous shareholders, armed with annotated copies of Sarbanes-Oxley and several thick volumes of the S.E.C.'s byzantine regulations. He'll be pissed if I interrupt him in the middle of such a proceeding, but then again, isn't this exactly why I was hired? How else is he going to know what his family is up to for the twenty hours a day that he's in the office?

It's settled. I'll do a special report. But first I've got to get some background, a bit of information, a little perspective. Why is Sheila crying? I decide to ask the girl, surely she'll have some insight into the situation. I look for her in the foyer. She's there, now engrossed in brushing the hair of some ditzy doll. I approach her, take a knee, ask her if she'll answer some questions. "My dolly is named Britney. She likes to eat cotton candy," she says. Jesus! Can we focus here for a minute? "This is important, Tanya. I need your help." Then, reminding me of why I can't stand kids, she says: "Britney's favorite snack is muffins, but she also likes salami." I take a deep breath, try to suppress my rage, imagine in my mind's eye the soothing expanse of the craps table, the rhythmic bouncing of the dice, the delirious smiles of the players collecting on frivolous bets. "Tanya," I say, exhaling, "may I please ask you something?" My sudden calm seems to grab her attention. "If I answer your dumb questions, will you play with me?" she queries. I agree to break the Journalism Academy's first principle to help me nail the story. "Yes," I say. "Yes I'll play with you. Now let's concentrate."

By the time I get my notebook back out and extend the lead a bit on the mechanical pencil, the girl is back to brushing the doll's hair so I take the doll away and pat it on the head and put it on the floor behind me. Tanya is clearly upset to lose her toy, but I'm not worried because this is no time for games. I look her in the eyes, impress upon her the importance of my inquiries. "Tanya, how long has your mother been smoking in the garage?" I ask. She looks diffidently at the floor, shuffles her feet. "I don't know," she says, "I guess since pancake time." *Pancake Time?* "You mean since you guys finished eating your pancakes?" "Yeah." "How long ago was that?" "I don't know. A long time ago?"

Another calming deep breath. I think back to the scene in the kitchen, figure from the degree of congealment on the breakfast plates that Sheila has probably been crying for at least an hour. If I had my chemical kit with me I could do a test or two and pinpoint the timing further, but this seems out of the question given the circumstances. In any event, the second question is by far the more important one. "Tanya," I say, "why is your mother crying in the garage?" She looks back at the floor, twirls a string of golden hair around an index finger. "I guess because Daddy is never around? She misses Daddy."

Of course! How come I hadn't thought of it earlier? If I had a wife who spent all day working at a big time law firm in the city while I stayed home watching the kids and doing needlepoint all day, I'd be sad too. And then if she hired a journalist to move in and report on everything we did all day so she could feel like she was staying informed about our family, well, then, hell, I don't know what I'd do. Freak out probably. Sit on the car and sob. Smoke a lot.

"Come on, Tanya," I say grabbing her little wrist and pulling her toward the staircase. "Come with me. We've got work to do. We've got to get your daddy back."

"But my dolly," she squeals. "What about my dolly?"

"Yes, indeed," I say, reaching back to grab Britney. "Good thinking. We're going to need that dolly."

In the makeshift web-casting studio my boss converted out of a spare den shortly before my arrival, I review my notes, draft up a rough outline of the report. I've put Tanya in a chair about six feet to my left. She is busy chattering to Britney about their plans to travel to the Serengeti this winter for tiger viewing and the like. Britney would rather follow some teen pop sensation around Europe, but she doesn't control the purse strings so she's out of luck.

I've changed for the occasion and now straighten my yellow tie with the turtles on it, the one that brought me no Pulitzers when I toiled for the Network. Pressing laptop keys in a pre-determined pattern, I kick the system into life. When I press CTRL-F3, the Special Report sequence starts up, and I know there's no going back. Somewhere, deep in the big city, in a mahogany boardroom appointed with crystal decanters and perhaps an oversized globe or two, my signal has now superseded the word processing program on the laptop computer that Robert Winston relies upon to remind him of certain facts and other particularities relevant to whatever controversy is currently occupying his attention. My boss is widely considered one of the best young litigators in the tri-state area, a hot shot recently elevated to partner a year before any of his peers at one of the town's top firms, but I happen to know that the secret to his success lies not in any sort of raw brains or God-given talent but rather in an ability to organize information into charts and columns and graphs and such that outstrips the organizational abilities of even some of the greatest organizers of this century or any other, including even perhaps the great Greek God Organysus, who of course gave the notion its very name.

The web-cam's red light goes on, I am live. I waste no time, forego introductions, skip the pleasantries. Not a word about the weather. I give it to him straight. First, the facts. His wife is bawling in the garage, has been there for an hour at least, according to estimates based on congealment of syrup, etc. She is wearing little makeup, no hair products, faded jeans, a sweatshirt that stinks of cigarette smoke. Next, the analysis. I indicate her refusal to answer questions, put forth my theory. She cries because you are absent, smokes to fill the void you leave. To bolster my case I point the web-cam to my left and pick up Tanya, who is still arguing with Britney regarding vacation plans. "Tanya," I interrupt, "Why does your mother cry?" "Daddy is missing," she says. "Tanya, what if you were daddy and Britney was your mother, what would happen?" Tanya crumples up her face and scowls at tiny Britney. "I'm leaving, I don't want you," she says, then heaves the doll with surprising force across the room into a relatively small but expensive piece of Intuit sculpture which falls off a dresser and cracks into two on the hardwood floor. I spin the web-cam around to capture the sad image of the busted statue. "There you have it," I say. "From inside the Winston home in this wealthy suburb of the big city, I am Andrew Tetley, and this has been a Special Report." I press CTRL-F4, and it's over and out.

Moments after the web-cam's red light goes off, my cell phone rings. It is Winston, and he is clearly troubled. "I'm canceling this deposition and coming home. Good work. Take the rest of the day off." Then, more faintly: "Goddammit, Johnson, we'll just have to reschedule for next week." He hangs up, and I exhale. For the first moment in the last two weeks, I am off the job.

Fifteen minutes later, it dawns on me that being off the job may not be so great. Perhaps I'd be more excited if I could go somewhere, but since I sold my used Camry months ago to pay off an ill-advised bet on a sub-par college football team whose mascot is some type of screaming cephalopod, leaving the house seems unlikely. I suppose I could walk the three miles to the local mall, but it is cold outside and my second-hand jacket is threadbare and I can't really afford to buy anything there anyway. Since I made a trip to the convenience store at the end of the street just yesterday, the small amount of cash I allot myself each week for frozen dinners, chocolate bars, etc. is already gone. For a second I contemplate calling a friend, maybe asking someone to come and take me away for the afternoon, but then I remember that since I moved two thousand miles to take this job, my friends are too far away to help, and I don't want to waste minutes chatting long-distance either. It would probably be worth it to speak with Stephanie, but she hasn't been much for talking ever since I lost our honeymoon money at a craps table while she was enjoying a bachelorette weekend with a group of friends at a hip luxury spa in the American Southwest.

The terms of my employment allow me full use of the house and its amenities, so I look around for something to occupy my time. I decide to stay away from the ground floor to avoid seeing Winston and his weeping wife, which leaves me the large second floor with all the bedrooms and the attic loft, complete with its well-stocked bar and exquisitely ornate full-sized oak pool table. The decision is obvious, and I settle in for an afternoon upstairs.

First thing's first, I pour myself a healthy glass of premium vodka over ice, garnish with two olives and an onion, suck it down, chomp the olives, gingerly nibble the onion. I pour another drink, grab the triangle, arrange the ivory balls in the appropriate striped-solid-alternating, yellow-ball-in-the-front, eight-ball-in-the-middle pattern that became second nature to me back when I practically minored in billiards my sophomore year of college. I remove the triangle, inch the rolling yellow-one-ball back to its rightful position at the apex of the pyramid, grip the cue. After a big sip and the obligatory twisting of the blue chalk cube on the cue's tip, I line up the shot. Looking down the cue stick's long shaft toward the perfect white ball at its end, feeling the stick's solid wooden weight in my right fist, imagining the cue ball sailing down the table toward its target and the resulting multi-colored explosion of numbered spheres, I feel a sudden sense of calm, perhaps the first such feeling I've experienced with my eyes open since I emerged from treatment. I stop and relish the feeling, smile, rest left cheekbone on shoulder and breathe. Returning my eyes to the table, I pull the cue stick back, release the trigger. The shot is just as I had imagined it. The balls ricochet with force, scatter to and fro. Several fall into pockets with satisfying thuds. I stand up straight, am exultant. It is going to be fine, I think to myself. It will all be all right.

This goes on for a long time, an hour, maybe two, shooting until all the balls but the cue have fallen, fixing another cocktail, resetting the table, repeat. On the stereo is playing a CD of a mildly famous eighties new wave band I'd long forgotten; I bop and skip around the table from shot to shot, push and pull the cue stick to the beat. It is as though I've entered some sort of chemically-based state of grace, the dopamine and synapses and serotonin all finally working together in pursuit of the same laudable goal. I cannot stop smiling.

And then I hear Winston's booming voice. He bellows my name, tromps up the stairs, probably two at a time. All at once the spell is broken, my joy dissipates into the room like a weak fart. I turn toward the staircase, frozen-faced await his arrival. As soon as his head appears above the balustrade, he turns and growls at me like an angry jungle cat, then bangs his fist over and over on the railing. "You dimwitted jackass," he blurts. "What the hell is wrong with you?"

Dimwitted jackass? Try as I might, I can't remember ever being called that before.

"Well?" he follows up, after I say nothing for about a minute. "Do you know what you did?"

"I'm sorry I ate seventeen olives."

"Not the olives, you dimwitted jackass, your special report."

There's that thing about the dimwitted jackass again. Why does that keep coming up? "What about my special report? Have you worked it out with Sheila? Agreed to stay home more often? One Sunday a month perhaps?"

This appears to make him even angrier. "She wasn't crying because I'm not around," he hollers. "She was crying because the man she's been having an affair with for the past six months called it off."

"An affair?" I query. "How could she be having an affair when she doesn't even leave the house after nightfall?"

"She leaves the house every single night, you idiot."

"Wait a minute," I say. "How could she be having an affair? Isn't she already married?"

And this is when I realize I'm tanked.

We are quiet for a long moment; Winston buries his face in his hands and rubs his temples. When his face emerges again, he speaks to me in a much quieter voice. "Did you do any behind the scenes investigation to find out why Sheila was crying? Any at all?"

I try to stay focused. Winston's face appears double, side-by-side, in my altered vision. "I talked to the little one," I squeak.

"Jesus," he says. "You are an awful journalist. Can you give me one reason—any reason at all—why I shouldn't fire you right now?"

I give his question some extended thought. If I had my notebook with me I would probably jot down some ideas, make an extended list, but I left the thing back in my bedroom and I doubt Winston would be much pleased if I stepped out to retrieve it. I cannot really think of anything persuasive to say. I could mention my training and experience, but the fact is he's right— I've never been able to pay much attention to detail, and this has always hindered my development as a newsman. I consider proposing that he keep me on as sort-of a day-nanny; I could play with little Tanya and her dolls, and maybe over time I could gain Sam's confidence, teach him some important values like generosity and perseverance. But then again, I hate children and don't really have any good values myself so what the hell's the point?

In the end, with my time clearly running out, I say the only thing that comes to mind. I tell him that I am protected by certain key contractual provisions, that federal law offers me rights and privileges as a full-time employee, that if he fires me I will sue him in a court of law. The stupidity of what I've said is clear to me as soon as the words leave my mouth, as they are also to Winston, who smiles and mockingly shakes his head, swivels and walks away, returns to his broken life below.

Reflections on the Distressed Fruit Series, Circa 1952

All oil paints and vinyl lettering on canvas, 1950-1952 by Jay Wexler

It's funny, because the *Art Forum* piece had just come out, I was in Stuttgart at the time, fielding so many interviews I can't really remember all of the many upstarts who came to see me, but there was one that has stuck with me these many years, I think she was a scholar from the countryside, and we were nibbling meat pies on the sidewalk, that much I certainly recall. Many of the comparisons had already been made at that point, to de Kooning and all the rest, but this one redheaded temptress insisted on probing the psychology of the matter and refused to even look at the goddamned paintings, those fruct-o-licious objects that had shaken the art world "like a Polaroid picture," as the kids say these days.

Swing music was blaring from the rooftops, and the papers were all a flurry with the news of the recent senatorial elections back in the States. This wasn't long after the war's end, after all, and yet the woman wouldn't shut up about my upbringing, the long-bared secrets of my early life frolicking with all those cousins on the outskirts of Lyón. She was smoking, I remember it clearly, and not one of those effete cigarettes so in vogue with the international art community at the time, no, no, this was practically a fucking cigar she was puffing on in between bites of mutton pastry and slurps of the local brew.

"Say something beautiful," she ordered me at one point, and I had no idea how to respond. Had I not said all I needed to say in the work itself? Everyone else seemed to think so, at least if you believed those at the editorial desks all over Europe and some of the more cosmopolitan areas of the American Northeast. She asked me if the works were an attempt at recovery. I told her that we are all recovering from something, aren't we, but she wasn't satisfied. When she started raising her voice and slapping her hands together like an apoplectic chimpanzee, I knew for sure that this was not your ordinary interview.

I had wanted to excuse myself and see to some business with the financiers because there were numbers to run and this talk was going nowhere, but before I could call for the bill, a young man who had been sitting to our left studiously poring over what looked like government reports on the escalating situation in Korea unceremoniously poked his bulbous schnozzle in our direction and demanded that my interrogator cease her cross-examination at once. It's been a long time, of course, and I cannot claim to remember everything that transpired in the ensuing minutes, but I can tell you for sure that blows were quite nearly exchanged that afternoon under the broadening shade of the glorious State Opera House.

Unsurprisingly, the dispute centered upon matters of high theory. You will remember, of course, that these were the days when entire volumes of *The Annals of British Aesthetics* were devoted to disputes over the existence of rainbows and their properties, so it shouldn't shock you to learn that color was also the focus of this particular amateur disagreement. The woman made the quite radical claim, one not generally adhered to by even the leading thinkers of this now entirely discredited school of thought, that colors are nothing, and that therefore she refused to consider the alleged tints of the fruit series as part of her review of the work.

Hogwash as it was, her eloquence and willingness to cite frivolously inapt sources in her defense had the unfortunate effect of driving my poor defender away from the practice of rational discourse and toward those baser instincts so prominently displayed in our contemporary attempts at "cultural production"—the soap operas, reality television, etc., etc. For my part, I was delighting in the scene now that I had drifted to its background; I continued to munch on the wonderfully spiced lamb offerings and even ordered an additional Spaten as the conflict threatened to spiral out of control. Both characters were out of their seats and a flamingo's elbow apart at the most; he was quite a bit shorter than she, and his stunning proboscis was practically buried in her ample bosom. The horn players on the café's rooftop stopped playing. The rising crescendo of the argument had long since eclipsed the Mingus tune they had commenced only moments before.

A fracas would have undoubtedly ensued if it hadn't been for the efforts of the local constable. A wiry man with an exquisite moustache and a linen uniform of periwinkle blue approached the scene with club outstretched, demanding information and an accounting of the circumstances. At once the situation defused. Identification was provided, apologies issued, vows of silence delivered, bribes handed over. The sudden re-emergence of the profane world in all of its flesh and substance, in the guise of this crisply dressed representative of the law, dispersed the ethereal disagreement like a puff of dust in the path of a typhoon.

The participants, humbled by the reprimand, settled their tabs and slinked away. The horns started up again. The café's other patrons returned to their papers, their croissants, their own affairs. I left too, and although I searched diligently over the coming months for the scholar's review, I found no trace of it. I doubt one was even published.

What Do You Like Best About Me?

Vera Salvaggio arrived on time for her 3:30 dentist appointment at the office of Dr. Robert Q. Smolover, DDS. Three hours earlier, after finally succumbing to the throbbing pain in her upper left molar that had been driving her mad for the past week, she decided to find herself a dentist right away, with no delay, on the double, at once, pronto, straight-away, forthwith, tout-de-suite. As a member of a health maintenance organization, she was then of course forced to choose a dentist randomly out of a book filled with men and women at the nadir of their profession, most of whom had gone to dental schools at places like the University of The Arctic Circle or the Chad School of the Dental Arts, to name two of the particularly strong ones. Armed with both pieces of information provided on each dentist by the HMO book, Vera decided that Dr. Smolover, who had at least attended a dental school in a developed nation and was somewhere between 24 and 84 years of age, would have to do the trick. Though she nearly gave up on the whole idea when Dr. Smolover answered the phone himself at his office by saying nothing but "hello," leading Vera to ask if she had indeed reached a dentist's office, to which Dr. Smolover had said simply, "uhh, yeah, I guess," the intense upper-molar pain impelled her onward to secure an appointment, which, it turned out, was easy to do, since Dr. Smolover hadn't had a patient since 1992.

When nobody answered her repeated knocks on the door, Vera let herself into Dr. Smolover's office. Vera decided that the place resembled more of a shoe repair store than a dentist's office; she reached this conclusion by observing that she was surrounded on all sides by shoes in various states of disrepair and shoe-repair equipment and a sign that said "Smolover's Shoe Repair" and also by noting the complete lack of a dentist's chair or a waiting room or any dental equipment of any kind. She looked around for the dentist tentatively, still mindful of the pulsating pain in her mouth and vaguely hopeful that somebody in this dusty shoe-strewn cavern could make the pain go away. "Hello?" she said. "Is anybody here? Dr. Smolover? I'm here for my 3:30. Hello?"

"Yeah, yeah, I'm right here," said a voice coming from a far away room. Vera waited for the source of the voice to enter the room she was standing in, but nothing happened. After waiting another minute or so, Vera ventured in the direction of the voice, opening door after door until she arrived in a small living room, outfitted with a fake Persian rug, two worn black leather couches, an outdated hi-fi system, a large black and white television with a round channel dial and no remote control, mountains of dust bunnies, and a full-sized dentist's chair with a working overhead light and spittoon-type contraption. A middle-aged man wearing a white coat was reclining in the dentist's chair smoking a cigarette.

"So, there you are. I thought you'd never fucking make it," said Dr. Smolover.

"Here I am," Vera responded, relieved to find that she apparently had made an appointment with a real live dentist. "But what type of dentist smokes and swears at his patients?" Vera wondered.

"Well, you gonna have a seat or what?" Dr. Smolover continued. "I ain't got all fucking day. I've got lots of shoes to put back together, you may have noticed."

"Oh, yes, of course I'll sit down," Vera said. "But, umm, right now you're in the dentist's chair. I'll just wait for you to get up. I mean, it wouldn't be appropriate for me just to sit down on top of you, now would it? How would you be able to examine my teeth and gums?"

"Oh, great, a goddamn intellectual," the dentist said, taking a long drag on his cigarette and blowing out a stream of smoke in Vera's direction. "I got Max fuckin' Weber over here."

"It's not really that I'm an intellectual," Vera responded. "I was just making a basic point about how it's impossible for one person to examine another person's teeth if both people are sitting on the...."

"Oh, shut your muffinhole already," Smolover blurted, rising slowly from the chair. "Just sit the hell down and open your muffinhole so I can take a look." The doctor crushed his cigarette out in an ashtray on top of the tray holding his various mirrors and scrapers and lit up another one.

Vera, unsure whether she was had made a terrible, terrible mistake, nonetheless took her position in the dentist's chair and waited for further instruction. "But what kind of dentist refers to a patient's mouth as a muffinhole?" she wondered.

"Well, you gonna open your muffinhole or what?" Dr. Smolover asked, approaching his fidgety patient.

Vera opened her muffinhole.

"All right, then, let's take a look." Smolover pulled a flashlight out of his coat and shined it at Vera's mouth. He looked up top and then down below. He studied her incisors and looked with great interest at her molars. He shook his head in disgust. "This shit's fucked up," he barked. He stood up, looked down at Vera with dismay, brought his cigarette to his lips, inhaled deeply, and blew a cloud of smoke into Vera's face. "They're gonna have to come the shit out," he announced.

Vera was shaken. "What do you mean, come out? Only one of them is giving me trouble. And why are you smoking? Is that right?"

"I'll tell you what's right and what's wrong," Smolover retorted. "Who do you think is the shoe repairman, I mean dentist, around here?"

"Uhh, you?"

"That's right. It's me. And I make the rules around here. You got that?"

Vera felt a painful twinge in her upper left molar and decided to submit to the dentist's authority. After all, he *had* graduated from the fifth best unaccredited dental school in all of North Dakota. "Yeah, I got that," she answered.

"Good," said the dentist. "I'm glad you have finally come around to see it my way after all this time." He stared at her for a few seconds and took a deep drag from his cigarette. He turned his head and blew the smoke out away from Vera's face. Vera was pleasantly surprised by this apparent newfound concern for her welfare on the part of the dentist.

"Can I ask you a question?" asked Smolover.

"I don't see why not," Vera replied.

"What do you like best about me?"

The question took Vera Salvaggio completely by surprise.

Vera had expected a question bearing on her dental condition. Perhaps something that inquired into her flossing habits, or brushing habits, or her choice in mouthwash. She also would not have been surprised if the question had concerned her eating habits, such as whether she ate a lot of sugar, how much celery she consumed, that sort of thing. And although it would have been a little odd if the dentist had asked her something about her dressing style, she would not have been nearly as surprised as she was by the question the dentist actually asked. For example, if the dentist had asked her whether she usually wore skirts (she was wearing one now) instead of pants, or whether she preferred natural fibers to artificial ones (she didn't), she would have been surprised, sure, but not so surprised as she was now.

"Uhh, umm, well," she muttered.

"It's not that difficult a question," Smolover retorted. "It is simple, straightforward. What do you like most about me? Is it my personality? My skills? My looks? My dental degree? The way my many leg hairs peep out between my nylon socks and my woolen pant leg?" He raised up his woolen pant leg to give Vera a peek at his black and bristly leg hair.

"Oh, no, it's not that," Vera exclaimed. "Sweet Jesus, it's not that."

"Well, then, what is it?" Smolover probed.

Vera tried to think of something. She looked up and down at this swearing, smoking dentist, and tried to figure out what she liked best about him. She didn't much like his looks. He was mustached and sort of creepy. She certainly didn't like his chair-side demeanor. And his dentistry credentials weren't tip-top either. So, what was it that she liked most about him? She thought about it a bit longer, and then it came to her.

"I like your participation in my health maintenance organization best!" she exclaimed.

Smolover stared sternly at Vera. He took a deep drag on his smoking stick and blew a cloud of smoke into Vera's face.

"What's wrong with my tennis shoes?" the dentist spat.

Vera coughed. "Can you please not exhale smoke in my face again?" she pleaded.

"What's wrong with my tennies?!" he asked again. "They're from the New Balance company, and they've got great insoles!"

Vera didn't really know what to do. She looked down at Smolover's feet. His sneakers were pretty natty, she had to admit. They were blue, with a nifty yellow design. They appeared to have excellent side support, and the fabric was impeccable. "But what kind of dentist asks what you like most about him, and then insists that you should like his sneakers best?" Vera wondered.

"What's it gonna be, Salvaggio?" inquired the dentist.

"Well, uhh," Vera muttered. "I guess your sneakers are very good. I suppose they are what I like best about you."

"Yes! Fucking A, YES!!!!" exclaimed the ebullient dentist, breaking suddenly into a wild Irish jig. "My tennies are the best, my tennies are the best," he sang.

Just then, a young and perky blonde woman threw open the door to the dentist's office and strode confidently inside. She took off her stylish black leather coat and laid it down over the arm of one of the leather couches before anyone could react to her presence. "Am I late?" she inquired harriedly. "I'm sorry if I'm late, Doctor Smolover."

"Oh, no, you're just in time," said the dentist. He turned to Vera and introduced the two women. "Vera, this is Katerina, my intern. Her favorite cheese is Muenster."

"Actually, I like Stilton just as much as I enjoy Muenster," Katerina said, outstretching her hand to shake Vera's. "Very nice to meet you."

"We've got a really interesting case here, Katerina," Smolover reported. "Would you like to take a looksie?"

"I'd love to," responded Katerina.

Katerina took the flashlight from Smolover and approached Vera. "Can you open up for me?" Katerina asked.

"Don't you want to say the word 'muffinhole'?" Vera asked.

"What?"

"Oh, uhh, nothing."

"I know what you're thinking," Katerina said, as Vera opened her mouth so Katerina could look inside. "You're probably wondering how come I can like both Muenster, which is a mild cheese, and Stilton, which is rather pungent."

Vera nodded her assent. She had thought the dichotomy was odd, although not really as odd as the fact that Katerina had brought the subject up at all.

"I'd explain it to you," Katerina said, looking carefully at all of Vera's gums and teeth. "I'm afraid, however, that I just don't want to."

"Mmmmm," Vera grunted.

Katerina fell quiet. She examined Vera's mouth for quite a while longer, periodically shaking her head in abject disgust. Finally, she stood up, sighed, turned toward the spittoon contraption at the side of the chair, hacked a few times, and spat a huge loogie onto the floor. "You're up shit's creek without a paddle, sugar blossom!" she exclaimed.

"What? Wait a minute," Vera replied. "I don't know what you're talking about. I just have one small tooth that's giving me a problem, and you're acting like I'm going to need a mouth transplant. Just where did you go to dental school, anyway?"

Katerina let out a robust guffaw. "Dental school?" Katerina asked through the laughter, "I think you've got it all wrong there, sister. I'm Doctor Smolover's shoe repair intern."

"Shoe repair intern?" Vera yelped.

"Yeah. That's right. And I'm damned good too. You should see what I can do with a worn out insole. I fixed those very sneakers on Dr. Smolover's feet right now for goodness sake. Now just sit back and relax. This will only hurt a bit." Katerina took a long needle from the tray and poured a hefty amount of a well-known antihistamine into its chamber.

Vera was crestfallen. Not only had she made a dental appointment with a smoking, swearing shoe repairman who hadn't worked on a dental patient in years, but she also had not even had the mental acumen to realize that Smolover's shoes were hand-me-down pieces of crap. What the hell was she doing, she wondered. Had things really come this far? Were Smolover's shoes really so worn down? She looked at Katerina with her enormous needle, and at Smolover, who had lit up another cigarette and was looking intently at a pair of purple pumps, and she figured that her life had become a joke. What should she do? Should she lean back and accept the quasi-oral surgery that it looked like Katerina was about to perform on her, or should she break out of her mental imprisonment and flee the scene without ever looking back? Time was running out, the needle coming closer. Vera closed her eyes..

"Open up," Katerina ordered.

Vera knew this was her last chance. She gathered her strength. She felt her wits returning to her. "No," she said, quietly.

"What?" said Katerina.

"Hold on a minute," said Smolover, dropping the pumps.

"You heard me," Vera said, sitting up in the chair. "I will not open my mouth. You two are not competent dentists. You are primarily shoe repair people. And I am not confident that you will adequately be able to treat my dental problems. I'm afraid that I'm just going to have to leave. Thank you for your help, but...."

"What?" interrupted Katerina, pulling back her needle. "You're not actually going to leave, are you? Did somebody hit you with a silly stick or something?"

"I cannot fucking *believe* this shit," bellowed Smolover.

Vera was taken back a bit by Smolover's outburst and by Katerina's reference to a "silly stick," whatever that was, but she had seen enough in the past fifteen minutes that she was no longer surprised by anything. "You better believe I'm leaving," she explained. "I just wonder why I didn't leave the minute I stepped foot in this place. I mean, you've got to be kidding me. You were just about to try to numb my teeth and gums with an antihistamine, for Christ's sake."

"You can't leave," Katerina said. "You've got an appointment. You have obligations to fulfill. You have responsibilities."

Smolover, meanwhile, started shaking uncontrollably with anger.

"What do you mean, responsibilities? My only responsibility was to show up for my appointment at the appointed time, which I did. I have no further obligations to you or to anyone else. I'm out of here."

"But this is a reciprocal relationship," pleaded Katerina. "There's *reciprocity* to deal with. What are you going to do about that? Do you have a plan for that?"

"SIT IN THE GODDAMNED CHAIR RIGHT NOW," screamed Smolover, jumping up and down. "SIT YOUR CABOOSE DOWN!"

"You can't just do whatever you want," Katerina added, a tear coming to her left eye, "just because you feel like it."

"PARK IT, CHIPMUNK!" screeched the dentist.

"There are rules in this world, you know," said Katerina, the tears seriously welling up now. "These rules exist to guide human behavior. And you are a human, so you have to follow the rules. You have to follow the rules because you are human."

"I WAS BORN ON THE MOON."

"I'm going to have to call the morality police on you," blubbered Katerina.

"MY UNCLE WAS A PANDA BEAR."

"All right, that's it," Vera said, heading for the door. "I'm going to report you to the better business bureau, or the American Dental Association, or the American Shoe Repairperson Association, or whatever the appropriate association is."

Smolover fell to his knees, dropped his cigarette, and grabbed his head with his hands. He shivered uncontrollably. He started weeping. The cigarette bounced off the implement tray, rolled on the floor, and came to rest by the door to the office, where it smoldered and sizzled like a smoldering, sizzling rolled up stick of tobacco.

Katerina wiped her tears and scowled at Vera, who had opened the door and was about to walk out into the hallway. "Will you look what you have done?" Katerina said. "I hope you're proud of yourself. I bet you think you're some big hero or something."

"Umm, I'll be seeing you later," Vera answered, with a dismissive wave of the hand.

"You're going to regret this some day," said Katerina, sitting down on the dentist's chair and pulling a piece of Muenster cheese from her pocket. "Someday you will regret what you have done here today. Someday you will be confined to the fires of hell for what you have done this afternoon."

Vera walked towards the door and stopped short at the sizzling cigarette. Realizing how dangerous it would be to leave a cigarette smoldering in an office full of such incredible lunatics, Vera stomped the thing out with her right foot, breaking her heel in the process. "Oh, damn," she exclaimed, taking off the shoe and looking disappointedly at its brokenness.

"Is anything wrong over there?" Katerina asked, shaking the slice of Muenster in Vera's direction.

"Umm, uhh, well, yeah," muttered Vera. She held the shoe towards Katerina. "Do you think you could take a look at this?" she asked.

"No," answered Katerina. "I don't know the first thing about shoes."

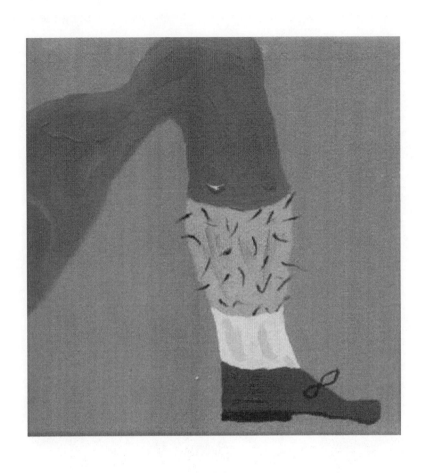

Clamming Camp

All this clamming is wiping me out. My legs are knee-deep in warm mud, my clam bucket only a quarter full. We've been going at it for hours, the hot summer sun baking my canvas-covered torso like a roast duck. I am twelve years old. My parents thought spending a few summer weeks at "clamming camp" would be good for me. They said I need to "learn of the sea's mystery," or some damned thing. We're not allowed to use the bathroom here during sunlight hours, so I let a little urine out into my pants and continue looking for clams.

The supervisor is a mustachioed clamming fanatic named Dunlop. He approaches with his whip raised high above his wavy coiffure of bright red hair and scowls. I shrink back a bit, and he grabs my bucket.

"What the hell is this crap?" he demands, rifling through the bucket's contents with his long, dirty fingers. "Scallop shells, bottle caps, nickels, Tootsie Rolls, a Lynyrd Skynyrd concert DVD? There isn't a damned clam in here anywhere. What the Christ have you been doing all morning, Talbot?"

He's right. I've been caught. I brought this stuff from home to fill the bucket. I can't clam worth shit. I don't know the first thing about finding or capturing any clams. But I don't want to suffer the relevant punishment either. So I make up a story.

"I'm sorry sir. I haven't located any clams yet. Suffering from diabetic-induced fibromyalgia and such. Feeling better though now, with the sun-induced vitamin D infusion, sir. Will bring my talents to bear on clam-digging starting pronto, etc."

Dunlop looks at me cross-eyed and with abundant suspicion. He's not buying the story, I can tell. After all, nothing in my application suggested any pancreatic ailment, and I lack any semblance of a doctor's note. "I'll be back in a half an hour," he blurts. "And if there aren't at least twelve clams in that bucket, you're going to Central for processing. I hear Lapizino is on call today, and he's recovering from cranial abrasions, so interactions won't be pretty." He cracks his whip a short distance from my left leg, and I wince. "Get to it. Hep, hep!"

Once he's gone, I catalog my options, weigh the costs and benefits, decide on a course of action. My decision: I will ask my friend Nachos what I should do.

Nachos, whose name was earned in connection with a cheese sauce eating incident too disturbing to report here, is standing on the fringes of the clamming bay surreptitiously reading his well-worn Penguin edition of The Brothers Karamazov. He's been reading this book continuously for the past three years, starting over on page one as soon as he finishes the final chapter. He claims to have completed the cycle twenty-eight times. When I approach him, I can hear him muttering insanely about the book's plot, its minor characters, its setting. "That Father Ferapont," he mumbles, "the barren Russian steppe!"

"Nachos," I exclaim. "Get your head out of that volume. I've got to discuss a pending matter with you."

Nachos looks up at me slowly and grins. He's got two rows of teeth like a shark, and his upper lip has bushy hair on both sides but is shaved in the middle, like some sort of reverse Hitler figure. "What is it, Talbot? I'm right in the middle of a dramatic sequence."

"It's fucking Dunlop again. He caught me loitering. I have no clams. The bucket is full of bric-a-brac, and I've got a half an hour to find twelve clams, or I'm heading down to Central, and rumor has it that Lapizino's got cranial abrasions."

He shakes his head, reflecting some combination of irritation at my interruption and pity for my situation. "Yeah," he acknowledges, "they say he took too many something-or-others and wasn't able to hold his own at the what not."

"I don't care the source of his displeasure," I reply, a bit of frustration seeping into my own voice. "I just need to figure out some way to get my hands on twelve clams in the next twenty-nine minutes or so, or it's the hot box for me. I'd get them through traditional clamming techniques, but I don't know any traditional techniques. What can you do to help?"

Nachos, who despite his nonchalant attitude and apparent indifference to the camp's central activity, is nonetheless a near-champion clammer, having taken seconds and thirds in mid-level clamming competitions up and down the east coast since he was old enough to tie his shoes. I can see him considering how best to respond to my plight. He's thinking something like: On the one hand it would be nice to give Talbot a few of my clams to get him out of this hot water with Dunlop so I can get back to my great Russian novel, but on the other hand if I could just teach this jackass how to clam for himself I wouldn't have to suffer these godforsaken interruptions every goddamned day. I can tell he is deep in thought because for ten minutes straight he is silent, scratching the top of his head with his left index finger, massaging his chin with right thumb and forefingers. In the meantime, I take the Lynyrd Skynyrd concert DVD out of my bucket and skim the liner notes. Time is precious, and it is slipping away. I have maybe eighteen minutes left before my fate is sealed. Impatience nearly gets the best of me when finally Nachos pipes up.

"Look, Talbot," he says, "here's the deal-ee-o." I hate when he talks like a twelve year old girl shopping for tight sweaters at the local mall, but in my desperate situation I have little choice but to suffer his painful diction silently. He continues. "I'm going to give you a few short lessons regarding clamming, and then you will be able to find sufficient clams to satisfy Dunlop not only today but every day, and then you won't have to interrupt my novel reading on a goddamned daily basis, OK?"

I had a feeling this was going to be his position. I am disappointed that he doesn't choose simply to hand me twelve of the three hundred or so clams he has collected in his own giant pail, but it's not like I don't see his point either. I nod, and we begin the lessons.

Before I know it, I am on all fours with my hands thrust into the warm mud up to my elbows. Nachos, who kneels next to me, is whispering secrets about intuiting the secrets of the clam, about uniting with the mystery of the sea. I try to follow his instructions, but I am having trouble locating even a single clam. At one point I think I have found one. I feel what seems to be a hard shell against my fingernail, but when I excavate the object it turns out to be only a large marble, delightfully pretty in its azure coloration but most certainly nothing that will satisfy Dunlop's bloodthirst.

To my right, Nachos has descended into some sort of ecstatic trance and is pulling up clam after clam, depositing each one in his now overflowing pail. My highly developed innate moral sense is the only thing that keeps me from thrusting Nachos' head under the mud and stealing his clams. I do my best to follow the lead of my champion caliber friend, but I know it is hopeless. A few minutes of futile grasping later, I heave my left arm out of the sludge and check my watch. My time is up. I look toward the horizon and see a rapidly advancing flash of red. As I imagine the fate that is in store for me, all I can do is hope and pray that Lapizino's cranial abrasions have begun to heal.

Confirmation Hearing of Sonia Sotomayor, if that Hearing Had Been Held in Front of the 1977 Kansas City Royals Instead of the Senate Judiciary Committee

George Brett [presiding]: Good morning. Welcome Judge Sotomayor, and congratulations on your nomination.

Sonia Sotomayor: Thank you very much. I'm delighted to be here.

George Brett: Let's get started, shall we? I will ask the first question. Much has been made since you were nominated about a speech you gave at Duke University, in which you suggested that the courts "create" the law. Some have charged that you will therefore be a so-called "judicial activist." In light of this speech, I wonder if you could comment on the propriety of the infield fly rule.

Sonia Sotomayor: Yes, of course. Wait a minute. What?

Larry Gura: And relatedly, please tell us whether you think it's right that a runner can tag up on a foul ball.

Sonia Sotomayor [consulting notes, flipping through them fruitlessly]: Yes, right, umm, infield fly rule. Tagging up. O.K. Just one moment....

Freddie Patek: I think what George and Larry are asking is whether you think it's OK for a grown man to cry. By himself. In a dugout.

John Mayberry [under his breath]: Pussy.

Sonia Sotomayor: Ahh, well, the Equal Protection Clause does give equal rights to men and....

George Brett: Perhaps we should change the subject a little. In his confirmation hearing a few years back, now Chief Justice Roberts analogized the role of the judge to the role of the umpire. Do you agree with that characterization. And specifically, do you think that it would be unconstitutional to waterboard Tim McClelland?

Sonia Sotomayor: I'm sorry. Tim McClelland?

George Brett: I'll phrase it another way. Let's say, for example, that a hypothetical rule prohibited the use of pine tar on any bat higher than eighteen inches above the tip of the handle. Would you "strictly construe" that provision as it applies to someone who has just hit a game winning home run?

Willie Wilson: And, also, would you legalize cocaine?

Hal McRae [muttering to himself]: Stupid questions.

George Brett [suddenly standing and wailing in pain]: Oh, my ass!

Sonia Sotomayor: If we could perhaps bring the discussion back to my constitutional theory?

George Brett [grabbing his ass]: Holy Chris Chambliss!

Hal McRae [still muttering]: Dumbassed questions.

Sonia Sotomayor: Perhaps I should mention that I once saved baseball?

U.L. Washington [chewing toothpick]: Why don't you tell us a little bit about that, Judge Sotomayor.

Sonia Sotomayor: Why, I'd be happy to talk about that case. And by the way, Mr. Washington, I've always wondered: what does the "U.L." stand for in your name?

[U.L. Washington stares silently at Sonia Sotomayor for, like, three whole minutes]

Sonia Sotomayor: Well, o.k. then.

George Brett [jumping up and down]: Sweet mother of Goose Gossage! [he leaves the room screeching]

Sonia Sotomayor: The case involved the 1995 player's strike against the owners. I ruled that the owners had violated the basic principles of collective bargaining and ordered the season to resume. The *Chicago Sun-Times* said that I had "delivered a wicked fastball" to the owners, ha ha ha, whatever that means.

Cookie Rojas: So, then, are you a baseball fan, Judge Sotomayor?

[At this point, Hal McRae starts totally freaking out]

Hal McRae [yelling like madman]: STOP ASKING ALL THESE STUPID ASSED QUESTIONS!! [Hal McRae starts throwing things like phones and shoes]. SAME STUPID ASSED SHIT EVERY SUPREME COURT NOMINATION HEARING. PUT THAT IN YOUR FUCKING PIPE AND SMOKE IT.

[silence]

Sonia Sotomayor: Hmm. That was odd.

Cookie Rojas: Don't mind him. He does that every hearing. You should have seen what he said to Ruth Bader Ginsburg. Please continue.

Sonia Sotomayor: I believe the question was whether I am a baseball fan. And yes, I would have to answer that in the affirmative.

Frank White: Terrific. That is a big point in your favor [makes checkmark on legal pad]. Now, where did you say you grew up again?

Sonia Sotomayor: In the Bronx. Bronx, New York.

[The entire bench erupts in angry disappointment]

Amos Otis: Oh, no.

Willie Wilson: Forget this.

Paul Splittorff: This can't be happening.

[The players get up to leave. On the way out, Hal McRae throws some more stuff toward Sonia Sotomayor. Afterwards, only Freddy Patek remains at the bench, quietly weeping]

George Brett [squeaking, from far away]: Ouch.

The Linear Apartment

Greta calls Bartholomew on her hand-held, and he responds immediately. Though in the midst of a landmark trial regarding the oft-deliberated but never quite resolved butterfly-moth distinction, he tells Greta to expect him in her Drumstead apartment by noon on Tuesday, if not before. Bartholomew plans to finish up closing arguments before dawn so he can grab a soil taxi and arrive on the Eastern Seaboard in time to make good on his promise. Having achieved fame in the mid-eighties by establishing conclusively that the tomato is neither fruit nor vegetable but fish, Bartholomew knows that he can be of great assistance to Greta in her landlord-tenant dispute. In any event, he's been in love with her forever, so he will do what he can to help.

Meanwhile, in the bathtub, Greta soaps herself up mightily. She likes to cover herself in bubbles and pretend to be a space alien. She rearranges her wool cap, pulls mittens tightly over dainty fingers. Adjusting her boots, she removes one of the three sweaters she has put on for the bath. She says "ninny, ninny, ninny" aloud to the empty room, because that's what she figures an alien might say. The water is warm, contrasting nicely with the brisk temperature of the room. She is happy that Bartholomew has agreed to come. It has been a long time since last they saw each other.

When they were kids, of course, they played typical children's games. One game was called "tip the rooster" and it was fun as all get out. One of them would count to ten and the other would think of a famous emperor from the Han Dynasty, and then they would discuss the ramifications. Often there were none, but that was half the fun.

As teenagers, they hung out with the in crowd, planted squashes to pass the time. Greta lettered in astronomy, while Bartholomew volunteered after school teaching marination techniques to under-privileged derelicts. Someone they now refer to as "that guy who screams 'Bam!'" was one of his first students. At the time, the guy couldn't pickle a cucumber, but now look at him there smiling on the vision cube with his mansions and big fat face and specialized equipment! Greta and Bartholomew dated on and off, shared hopes for the future, tickled each other until their livers shattered with joy. It was dreamy.

But Bartholomew had left soon after graduation, first to Africa and then to Vegas to study rhetoric and enter the learned professions, while Greta remained in Southern Indiana scraping and scratching the fertile dirt with metal detectors and dreaming of a life out east. They had traded letters, missives, and other communications trapped in empty bottles, but had rarely spoken and only seen each other once, in Detroit during Bartholomew's leave from the war, when there was little time to discuss matters of the heart or anything else. Soon after, Greta applied for the position she holds now as assistant doppelganger at a semi-prominent Tex-Mex chain in Drumstead. Maryland might not have been her first choice, but it has served her well, and these days she sometimes even goes weeks without wanting to off herself with the crude, self-fashioned guillotine she keeps in her bedroom, just in case.

She had married once, but the marriage hadn't lasted long. Its disintegration had started with the kittens. She remembered when they purchased the first one, a sickeningly cute chocolate purebred with five legs that pouted like a spoiled child when deprived of her favorite toy—a marionette in the shape of the abominable snowman that spoke one of several pat phrases when his tail was pulled briskly. She and Rex had fought endlessly over that damned kitten, and when they decided to buy two more, Greta knew that the end was near. The calico was needy and the Maine Coon was a bastard-and-a-half, to say the least. The stress that care of the kittens placed on the marriage was too much, especially with the children and their special needs (the young one a halfwit, the older a preternaturally precocious intellect with a disposition towards forensic science and a maddening obsession with bells of all shapes and sizes) and the demands of the workplace, particularly Rex's position as a crab measurer which required his presence almost continuously at the docks, where he was known as "the great measurer," an appellation that, frankly, drove Greta out of her fucking skull.

It will be nice, Greta figures, to see Bartholomew again.

* * *

It is mid-afternoon on Tuesday when Bartholomew finally arrives on Greta's doorstep. The trial has lasted longer than expected, and so he is late. The proceedings were going fine until the judge, frustrated by the issue's complexity and his own lack of legal training, issued contradictory injunctions and sent the jury to bed without dinner. Bartholomew is expected back in the courtroom on Thursday, so he won't have much time to resolve Greta's landlord-tenant dispute. Meanwhile, Greta, nervous that Bartholomew might not show, has knitted herself a sweater to pass the time but since the arms were of different lengths she has already reserved a slot at the Salvation Army's next bake sale. When Bartholomew rings the doorbell, Greta is busy practicing her sitar, but no matter how many times she works through "Smells Like Teen Spirit," she cannot get it to sound right.

As soon as Greta lets Bartholomew in through the front door, the two ex-lovers fall immediately into their old routines, as though thirteen long years had not passed since last they met. They tickle each other gently under moist armpits and quiz each other on various ancient emperors. "Emperor Huang!" exclaims Greta, and they both agree that there are no relevant ramifications.

Bartholomew understands Greta's problem immediately. The apartment is linear. It makes no moves. It takes no turns. It is straight as the proverbial arrow. Together the friends stand in the kitchen, their backs against the refrigerator, and look directly out over the breakfast bar, into the living room, through the French doors that separate the living space from the bedroom, and out the window on the far wall that overlooks the busy street below. "Why, this is the most linear apartment I have ever seen!" Bartholomew yelps. Greta is elated that someone has finally understood the thorn that has stuck in her side for so long. "Now you understand why I had to put the kids up for adoption," she answers.

Before too long, Bartholomew finds himself sitting at the kitchen table, immersed in the legal particularities of the case, leafing through documentation, preparing interrogatories, developing strategies for manipulating his enemy. "What did you say your landlord's name is again?" he asks. "Carson," Greta answers. "Well, I'll tell you what," Bartholomew says, practically cackling with nefarious delight. "This Carson's ass is grass, and I'm the weed whacker, heh, heh, if you know what I mean." Greta has no idea what he means, but she smiles warmly anyway. Someone, after all, has finally agreed to lend her a hand.

* * *

The meeting with Carson does not go as smoothly as Bartholomew hoped. For one thing, Carson thinks the whole notion of a "linear apartment" is a load of shit.

"What do you mean, the apartment is linear?" he asks. "Are you nuts?"

Bartholomew has prepared for this objection. He aims a quick smile over at Greta, who is knitting a varsity jacket at the far end of the conference table the three have arranged themselves around, and then he turns back to face Carson. "No, I'm not nuts," he answers in the mocking sing-songy voice that he reserves for moments just like this. He picks up his fist and brings it quickly back down towards the table, stopping just short of contact, placing the fist softly on the surface, his trademark gesture that sends shivers of fear through most of his opponents in the Midwest, but which does not seem to faze Carson in the least. The landlord ignores the attorney and continues picking through a box of peanut M&Ms, eating only the green ones and opening his mouth in mid-chew in an attempt to gross out his adversary.

A longtime veteran of many hard-fought litigation battles, Bartholomew is not distracted by Carson's shopworn tactics. Instead, he focuses on the task at hand, opens and closes several file folders, lays out Greta's prima facie case. First, the facts. The apartment is too straight. There are no turns. More angles are needed. Curves must be introduced. Next, the legal theory. The lease, Bartholomew points out, referring to a copy which he has highlighted with several neon-hued markers, requires certain minimum conditions of habitability, guarantees quiet satisfaction of the premises, ensures enjoyment of the same. Finally, application of the law to the facts: The apartment's linearity is undermining his client's living pleasure. She takes turns and runs into walls, cancels dinner parties out of shame, is haunted by the directness of it all. Bartholomew slams shut his day planner. "And that's our case. Shall I mark you down as offering your concession now, or would you like an extra minute to think about it?"

Carson looks over at his tenant and her counselor in disbelief. He stands up half way out of his chair and snatches the lease that Bartholomew is holding in his left hand. The landlord looks over the provisions quickly and shakes his head disapprovingly. "Look, I don't know what you think you're doing here, but there is nothing in this lease that prohibits me from renting your client an apartment that goes in a straight line." Carson throws the lease back down on the table and returns his buttocks to the seat below. "And in any event," he blurts, "what would you have me do about it?"

"Aha!" belches Bartholomew, opening up a file folder labeled "Redress." He flips through a few torn pieces of notebook paper, excerpts from an unpublished legal treatise he penned in the waning years of a prior decade. "We will undoubtedly be seeking remedies commensurate with the injury," he says. "Relief will be pursued, several notions are being mulled over, of course we shall be seeking attorney's fees in addition to other forms of restitution, pursuant to the Restatement Fourth on Declaratory Judgments, among other things."

"Fuck this shit," Carson blurts, standing up and tossing an M&M in Bartholomew's general direction. "I'm out of here." The door shuts behind Carson just moments after the M&M bounces off of Bartholomew's head and tumbles to the conference room floor.

* * *

The lovers are back in Greta's apartment, packing her belongings into cardboard boxes marked with Bartholomew's Midwestern address. Bartholomew has not succeeded in helping Greta with her landlord-tenant dispute, but he has solved her problems nonetheless. The two pack silently, lost in their own thoughts, occasionally untying each other's shoelaces just for the fun of it. Bartholomew has been eager to abandon his bachelor life-style for many years now, and he looks forward to the change with great anticipation. Greta is excited too, but she feels bad about quitting her job without giving the requisite two weeks' notice. The assistant manager was incensed, threw quesadillas on the ground in disgust, threatened to take out defamatory advertisements in several Ohio newspapers. Greta knows he will recover, but she also understands that the vision of her boss's contorted face streaked with tears will remain in her memory long after she has departed the Atlantic coast.

Greta hears Bartholomew's voice bellowing from the bedroom. He has found the guillotine and wants to know whether to pack it up in one box or two. "Leave it," she says. "I won't be needing it any longer." Then under her breath: "I can always build another one if that's what it comes to."

—————— ✿ ——————

"Death Row"

A Situation Comedy

Pilot Episode:

"Rusty's Last Day"

FADE IN

INT. PRISON STAFF ROOM - MORNING
(JED, GEORGE, SALLY, TRENT, RUSTY)

THE ROOM WHERE THE PRISON STAFF CONGREGATES IS LARGE
AND CONTAINS MANY DESKS AND FILE CABINETS. A SIGN AT
THE ENTRANCE READS "APPLETON CORRECTIONAL FACILITY: IF
YOU'RE ON DEATH ROW, YOU'VE COME TO THE RIGHT PLACE."
THE CLOCK ON THE WALL READS 8:00. GEORGE, A GUARD
WHO HAS SEEN IT ALL, SITS NEAR THE COFFEE MACHINE
DRINKING A CUP OF COFFEE AND READING THE PAPER. JED,
THE PRISON'S GRIZZLED EXECUTIONER, ENTERS WEARING A
LONG WHITE COAT AND HOLDING TWO OPEN BEAKERS FULL OF
COLORFUL LIQUID.

                    JED
        Morning, George. Big day ahead of
        us today, eh?

                    GEORGE
        That's putting it mildly. I can't

                    91

believe ol' Rusty is finally
getting the lethal injection. Never
thought I'd see the day. He's been
here 20 years, almost as long as I
have.

JED APPROACHES THE COFFEE MACHINE TO GET A CUP, BUT
REALIZES HE DOESN'T HAVE A FREE HAND TO POUR THE
COFFEE.

JED

(extending one of the
beakers to George)

Hey, George, will you hold this for
a minute?

GEORGE

(taking the beaker)

Oh, yeah, sure. No problem.

JED BEGINS POURING HIMSELF A CUP OF COFFEE.

GEORGE (CONT'D)

(examining the beaker)

Hey, Jed, what is this stuff,
anyway?

JED

Oh, that? That's sodium pentothal.
I'm gonna need that for the lethal
cocktail tonight.

GEORGE

(shocked, he drops the
beaker on the floor)

Geez, Jed. You can't go handling
people hazardous substances without
a warning.

JED

Oh no, George. Now look what you've
done. Where am I going to get some
more sodium pentothal for the
execution? I guess I'm going to

have to go out to the WalMart on
Route 46, that'll take me over an
hour.

                    GEORGE
        (getting some paper towels
        and starting to clean up)

I'm sorry, Jed. I didn't mean it.
You just took me by surprise. I'll
clean this up. Hey, this burns a
little.

                    JED

Oh, don't worry about it. It isn't
your fault. It's just this lethal
injection stuff is so complicated.
I haven't even figured out what
exactly I'm supposed to put in this
cocktail. Things didn't used to be
this complex. Back in the day, you
just pulled the switch and sizzle,
sizzle, that was it. I mean, sure,
sometimes the guy didn't quite lose
consciousness for half an hour,
but, hey, them's the breaks.

                    GEORGE
        (looking at his hand, now
        smoking)

Do we have any aloe vera gel around
here somewhere?

SALLY, THE PRISON'S CHEF, ENTERS WEARING A LARGE WHITE
CHEF'S HAT AND CARRYING A STACK OF COOKBOOKS.

                    SALLY

Good morning, everyone.

                    JED

Hi Sally.

                    GEORGE

Hey there, Sally. What's with all
the books?

SALLY
(putting the stack down with
a thud)

They're cookbooks. I've finally
got the chance to make a real final
meal around here, and I'm going to
make Rusty something he'll never
forget. Well, I guess that's not
the right choice of words, but you
know what I mean.

GEORGE

I'm not sure, Sally. I've known
Rusty for twenty years, and all
that time he's talked about how he
wants his final meal to be a simple
cheeseburger, fries, and a coke
from McDonald's.

SALLY

Oh, no way. I didn't get my degree
at the Culinary Institute of
America, spend six months studying
in Paris under the best chefs in
the world, and make grilled cheese
lunches here for five years waiting
for a chance to make one four star
final meal that would get me on the
Food Network just to buy this guy a
McDonald's cheeseburger. No, sir.
This guy's having the meal of his
life tonight. (PAUSE) So to speak.

SALLY LEAFS THROUGH ONE OF THE COOKBOOKS.

SALLY (CONT'D)

Hmm, maybe he'd like some Coquille
St. Jacques. Perhaps a nice arugula
salad. I wonder if he likes sushi.

GEORGE

He's never going to go for it.
Rusty is a steak and potatoes guy,
nothing fancy about him.

SALLY

Look, who's this about? Him or me?

TRENT ENTERS. TRENT IS THE PRISON'S WARDEN, A LARGE, MIDDLE AGED, ATTRACTIVE MAN WHO DEEPLY BELIEVES IN THE JUSTICE OF THE DEATH PENALTY AND THE IMPORTANCE OF HIS JOB, EVEN THOUGH HE HAS DEVELOPED SOME ADMIRATION FOR A FEW OF THE INMATES.

TRENT

Everyone ready for the big day?

JED

(surfing the web)

Hey, boss, do you know exactly what goes into this lethal injection?

TRENT

What? Are you kidding?

JED

No. I'm trying to find some information on the world wide web here, but I'm not good with computers. I know that one of the poisons is supposed to stop the kidneys. Or is it the lungs?

TRENT

You mean you've been sitting around this prison for five years waiting for our first execution and you haven't prepared for it at all?

JED

Hey, I've had a lot of solitaire to play. Now are you going to help me here or what?

TRENT

I don't know the first thing about chemicals. That's your job. And you better figure it out by midnight, that's all I've got to say. Everything else around here ready to go?

                    SALLY

Boss, do you think that Rusty
would enjoy a nice dish of poached
Chilean sea bass topped with a red
pepper and cilantro coulis? With a
side of baby carrots and artichoke
infused cous cous?

                    TRENT

(looking at Sally in disbelief,
then at George)

Is she serious?

                    GEORGE

I don't know, boss. But everything
looks like it's ready to go.
Father McConnell should be over
sometime after his three martini
breakfast to get Rusty ready to
meet his maker, and we're expecting
Spaulding, Rusty's court appointed
lawyer, any time now. I guess
they're going to file one last
appeal with the Supreme Court.

                    TRENT

Well, good luck with that. The
Court almost never stays an
execution. And that's when the
prisoner has a lawyer with actual
criminal training. This Spaulding,
what is he, a tax lawyer or
something?

                    JED

Remember when Spaulding filed that
tax return with the appeals court
instead of a brief?

                    TRENT

(shaking his head)

Poor Rusty never had a chance.

                    SALLY

Do you think he would enjoy a
Baked Alaska for dessert? But then
again, that could take a while to
make. Hey, boss, can we delay the
execution to like one a.m.?

                    TRENT

Are you serious?

                    SALLY

You're right. Better make it two
a.m.

SALLY LEAVES.

                    JED

    (finding something on the
    web and scribbling on a pad
    of paper)

Aha! Here it is. "How to Make a
Lethal Cocktail." Hmm, let's see.
Ingredients. Sodium Pentothal,
Demoral, Morphine, and Immodium.
All right, I think I've got it.
I just have to go pick up a few
things. I'll be at WalMart, but
I'll be back by lunch. Don't
execute anyone without me. Ha,
ha. Get it? You can't execute
anyone without me. Because I'm the
executioner. Get it?

                    TRENT

What's he talking about? What's
going on around here?

GEORGE LOOKS AT HIS HAND, WHICH IS NOW BRIGHT RED AND
SLIGHTLY ON FIRE.

                    GEORGE

Hey, Jed. Do you think you could
pick me up some bandages while
you're out?

                          TRENT
              (giving up on figuring out
              his employees and turning
              his attention to a file)
          George, is today the day that the
          new guy shows up?

                         GEORGE
          Who, Harry Harrison? Harry Harrison
          who killed his whole family with an
          ordinary office stapler? You bet.
          They're bringing him here sometime
          before lunch. Should I put him in
          Cell Four?

                          TRENT
          Is that the cell that Johnny was
          in before those pesky DNA experts
          quote unquote exonerated him?

                         GEORGE
          No, Johnny was in Cell Six. You
          know, the solitary confinement
          cell with no lights and all the
          poisonous spiders? Marvin was in
          Cell Four. That was before the real
          murderer confessed to the police
          after twenty-five years.

                          TRENT
          Oh, yeah. That's right. I remember
          he had this portable television
          and everyone gathered around to
          watch Reagan's first inauguration.
          Anyway, I guess Cell Four will be
          fine for Harrison.

FROM OUTSIDE THE PRISON, THE SOUND OF LOUD PROTESTING
AND CHANTING IS HEARD.

                      TRENT (CONT'D)
          What is going on out there?

TRENT AND GEORGE LOOK OUT THE WINDOW. THEY SEE A
LARGE CROWD PROTESTING THE IMMINENT EXECUTION. THE

PROTESTORS HOLD SIGNS AND CHANT. THEY ARE LED BY
<u>STEPHANIE</u>, AN ATTRACTIVE AND HEADSTRONG WOMAN IN HER
MID-30S WHO IS AN ARDENT ANTI-DEATH PENALTY ACTIVIST.
SHE IS WHIPPING THE CROWD OF PROTESTORS INTO A FRENZY,
IN FRONT OF A LINE OF TELEVISION CAMERAS.

> TRENT (CONT'D)

Oh, great. We're going to have to
put up with this all day.

> GEORGE

And I heard they're planning a
candlelight vigil for midnight too.

> TRENT

Terrific. Just what we need, a
bunch of mamby pamby ACLU liberals
who don't understand anything about
anything making our life difficult.

> GEORGE

They are just exercising their
first amendment rights.

> TRENT

First amendment, shmirst amendment.

> GEORGE

Yeah, good point.

> TRENT

She is pretty cute though.

> GEORGE

What?

> TRENT

Oh, nothing.

FROM THE ADJACENT CELLBLOCK, LOUD VOICES ARE HEARD.

> RUSTY (O.S.)

All I want is a cheeseburger and
fries.

                    SALLY (O.S.)
        But I studied at the Culinary
        Institute of America. I spent six
        months in Paris.

                    TRENT
        Oh, not again.

                                        CUT TO:

                    ACT ONE

                    SCENE B

INT. CELLBLOCK-MOMENTS LATER
(RUSTY, SALLY, WINSTON, PATRICIA, GEORGE, HARRY, GARY)

NEXT TO THE LARGE ROOM WHERE THE PRISON STAFF
CONGREGATES IS THE PRISON'S SMALL CELLBLOCK. THE
CELLBLOCK HOLDS FOUR CELLS, THREE OF WHICH ARE
CURRENTLY OCCUPIED. IN ONE CELL IS RUSTY, AN AFRICAN-
AMERICAN MAN IN HIS EARLY SIXTIES WHO HAS BEEN ON
DEATH ROW FOR OVER TWENTY YEARS AND IS PRACTICALLY
LIKE FAMILY WITH THE PRISON STAFF. A SECOND CELL HOLDS
PATRICIA, A SHORT, WHITE-HAIRED OLD LADY WITH GLASSES
WHO IS THE STATE'S ONLY FEMALE DEATH ROW INMATE. IN
THE THIRD CELL IS WINSTON, A 1972 GRADUATE OF HARVARD
LAW SCHOOL, WHO IS PRESENTLY QUITE INSANE. SALLY IS IN
FRONT OF RUSTY'S CELL, TRYING TO CONVINCE HIM TO LET
HER MAKE A GOURMET FINAL MEAL.

                    RUSTY
        I don't care if Francois Mitterand
        presented you with the Legion of
        Honor, I don't want foie gras
        stuffed prunes for my last meal
        on this earth. I haven't had a
        McDonald's cheeseburger for twenty
        years, and that's what I want for
        my final dinner.

SALLY

I just don't understand. I'm
offering to make you a delicious
gourmet meal that you could only
get by paying over a hundred
dollars in a trendy New York
restaurant, and you want a fast
food meal that anyone could get in
any tiny town in the country for
less than three dollars.

RUSTY

But that's just the point, don't
you see? Anyone can get that meal,
except for me. And I've been
craving it for two decades.

SALLY

What am I supposed to tell the Food
Network guys? They're supposed to
be here any minute to start filming
my preparation for their "Save the
Best for Last" special. That was
going to be my ticket to a real
chef's job in a real restaurant.

RUSTY

Look, I know you're still
disappointed that this prison
chef job was the only chef's job
you could land after all your
fancy training, but this meal is
about what I want, not about what
you want. If it will make you
happy though, you could have them
supersize my fries.

SALLY

Ugh.

WINSTON

Pineapples are one of my favorite
vegetables, though rutabagas come
in a close second.

SALLY

Winston, we're not talking about
pineapples right now.

WINSTON

My mother was, in some important
respects, a koala bear.

PATRICIA

Oh, for goodness sakes, Winston,
can't you control your raging
insanity for just one day? Give
poor Rusty a break on his last day,
won't you?

WINSTON

His ears were fluffy, and he ate
mostly eucalyptus leaves.

SALLY

So this is your final decision?

WINSTON

Not exclusively eucalyptus, but
mostly.

RUSTY

I'm afraid it is.

SALLY

Fine. Have it your way. How many
ketchup packets do you want with
those fries? You want salt?

PATRICIA

Hey, while you're arranging to
take care of our basic needs, could
you find out what happened to my
Soldier of Fortune subscription?
I haven't gotten an issue in
months. I have to keep up on the
new developments in assault weapon
technology. You know, just in case
my appeal goes through.

SALLY

Forget it. That subscription was
taken away for a good reason.

PATRICIA

Hey, nobody actually proved I was
running an international weapons
syndicate from my jail cell. And
anyway, that thing's been shut
down ever since Yuri was nailed by
Interpol.

GEORGE ENTERS, HIS INJURED HAND WRAPPED IN ICE,
LEADING NEW PRISONER HARRY WITH HIS OTHER ARM.

GEORGE

All right, Harrison. Say hello to
your new home for the rest of your
life.

HARRY

Oh, I won't be here long. I'm
actually innocent. My lawyer is
confident about my case, so I'll
probably be out of here in a week
or two.

GEORGE

Oh, is that right?

HARRY

Yeah, so if it's OK, you don't
have to put me with all the real
criminals. You know, if you can
just put me in the, uhh, the
innocent section of the prison,
that'd be great.

GEORGE

Oh, sure. Of course. The innocent
wing. Right this way.

PATRICIA

Hey, who's the new guy?

GEORGE

Patricia, everyone, this is Harry
Harrison. He was convicted of
killing his whole family with an
office stapler. But you probably
don't want to invest too much time
getting to know him, because he
informs me that he's innocent, so
he won't be staying long.

RAUCOUS LAUGHTER ALL AROUND.

PATRICIA

Innocent, huh? Yeah, I'm innocent
too. Aren't you innocent, Rusty?

RUSTY

Oh, yes. Yes, maam. Innocent as a
newborn babe.

WINSTON

I'm innocent. Innocent as a newborn
blueberry.

GEORGE

Well, Harry. Looks like this is
your lucky day. It appears that
everyone here is innocent. So you
should fit right in. Here you go,
Cell Four. All the amenities. Desk.
Cot. Two foot by two foot window.
Toilet. Enjoy.

GEORGE PUSHES HARRY IN HIS CELL AND LOCKS IT.

HARRY

No, I don't think you understand.
I'm really innocent.

GEORGE

(giggling)

Really innocent. That's a good one.

GEORGE LEAVES. HARRY LOOKS AROUND AND NOTICES EVERYONE
SEEMS DEPRESSED.

HARRY

Hey, what's everyone looking so
down for?

PATRICIA

Today is Rusty's execution day.
He's only got fifteen hours left to
live.

HARRY

What? You mean, they actually
execute people around here?

RUSTY

What'd you think this place was, a
country club?

HARRY

Well, I never thought they'd really
go ahead and kill someone. Good
thing my lawyer's going to get me
off.

RUSTY

Yeah, right.

PATRICIA

Speaking of lawyers.

GARY, RUSTY'S INCOMPETENT LAWYER, ENTERS. HE IS
RUMPLED AND FRAZZLED. HE CARRIES A MESSY STACK OF
PAPERS, FILES, AND BOOKS.

RUSTY

Hey there, Spaulding. I sure hope
you've figured something out
that'll stop my execution.

GARY

(dropping the pile of stuff)

You know, I think I may have
identified a theory that could be
of some help.

                    RUSTY

That's great. Let's hear it.

                    GARY

Well, I've just started working on
it. But I'm sure that with a little
more research, I'll definitely be
able to whip something together by
next month.

                    RUSTY

What? Next month? But they're going
to execute me tonight.

                    GARY

    (looking at his watch)

Are you sure?

                    RUSTY

Yes, I'm sure. I think I would
know.

                    GARY

Well, then. I guess we better get
started. (FUMBLING AROUND IN HIS
POCKETS). Anyone got a pencil?

RUSTY DROPS HIS HEAD INTO HIS HANDS IN DESPAIR.

                    ACT II

                    SCENE A

INT. CELLBLOCK-THREE O'CLOCK
(RUSTY, GARY, WINSTON, PATRICIA)

ON A TABLE SET UP OUTSIDE RUSTY'S CELL, GARY HAS
SPREAD OUT LEGAL BOOKS AND PAPERS. HE IS DISHEVELED
AND IS CLEARLY DESPERATE. RUSTY SITS INSIDE HIS CELL
TRYING TO HELP GARY, BUT HE TOO IS LOSING HOPE.

                    RUSTY

We've been working for hours now,
and you still haven't figured

anything out for our final appeal.
It looks like I'm doomed.

GARY

Now, now. Don't panic. I think
you're right that we don't really
have any more state law arguments.
(PICKS UP BOOK AND LOOKS AT THE
SPINE). We are in Virginia, right?

RUSTY

Oh boy.

GARY

But maybe we could make an argument
based on the federal Constitution.
I think there are some important
amendments in that. Now, what
were they again? (PICKS UP ANOTHER
BOOK). Something about illegal
searches or something.

RUSTY

Did you even go to law school?

GARY

Yes, I went to a law school. It
might not have been (MAKES AIR
QUOTES) accredited, but I did pass
the bar and can practice in several
states. I'll even be able to
practice in New York again once my
(MORE AIR QUOTES) probation period
is over.

RUSTY

So how come you don't know what the
Constitution says?

GARY

Hey, I'm a tax lawyer. I can't
help it if the court appointed me
to challenge your execution even
though I've never worked on a
criminal case before in my life.

It's not like lawyers are lining
up to take capital cases for nearly
no money. I mean, if you'd like to
hire Johnny Cochran, I can get you
his number. I'm sure he doesn't
charge too much. Plus, he's dead.

                    RUSTY

All right, all right. Let's think.
Hey, can't we argue that it was
illegal for the police to search my
house without a warrant?

                    GARY

Well, that would be a good
argument, but I'm afraid we waived
that one when I didn't argue it on
appeal in the lower court.

                    RUSTY

Oh, you mean when you filed the tax
return instead of my brief?

                    GARY

Look, I've apologized for that
already. I don't know what else you
want from me.

                    WINSTON

Why don't you argue ineffective
assistance of counsel? Violation
of Rusty's sixth amendment rights.
Spaulding was incompetent for not
filing the brief. Strickland versus
Washington.

                    GARY

What?

                    RUSTY

Oh, don't pay any attention to him.
He's crazy.

                    GARY

No, that's a great idea. Why didn't
I think of that?

WINSTON

Because you're incompetent?

GARY

Yes. That's right. I'm completely
incompetent. How could anyone be
put to death if they're represented
by someone as unfit and inept as
myself? That's what I'm going to
argue. I think this just may work.
Hey, how did you come up with that
idea?

PATRICIA

It's a little known fact that
Winston graduated magna cum laude
from Harvard Law School in 1972.
Of course that was before he went
nuts and hacked up the Lieutenant
Governor.

GARY

Wow. Who would have guessed it?
Ineffective assistance of counsel.
Great idea. Hey, what was that case
you mentioned again?

WINSTON

I was born on Neptune.

GARY

Never mind. I'll find it. All
right, I better get back to my
office and write this up if I'm
going to get it to the Supreme
Court on time. You just sit tight.
I'll be back later this evening. I
think we might have some hope.

GARY GATHERS HIS MATERIALS AND LEAVES.

RUSTY

Nice job, Winston. Thanks.

WINSTON

I'm my own father you know.

                                        CUT TO:

ACT II

SCENE B

INT. PRISON STAFF ROOM - SIX O'CLOCK
(JED, GEORGE, SALLY, TRENT, PATRICIA, MCCONNELL)

IN THE STAFF ROOM, GEORGE SITS AT HIS DESK EXAMINING
HIS BANDAGED HAND. SALLY IS AT HER DESK WITH HER
HEAD ON THE DESK. JED IS AT HIS DESK MIXING VARIOUS
CHEMICALS IN DIFFERENT BEAKERS AND CONSULTING THE
COMPUTER FOR GUIDANCE.

                    JED

        OK, I think I might have it. Two
        parts sodium pentothal, one part
        Immodium, one part blue food
        coloring. Then add this mixture,
        and that's it. I sure hope this
        works. I guess we won't really know
        until midnight, though, will we? We
        didn't have this problem back when
        we used the noose. I mean, sure
        sometimes the guy would just hang
        there for a half an hour before he
        suffocated, but hey, them's the
        breaks.

                    GEORGE

        My hand is killing me. Jed, do you
        have any chemicals over there that
        might numb this pain? Those six
        aspirins didn't seem to help.

                    JED

        Oh, sure. Let's see, I think the
        Demoral should do the trick. Here,
        drink this (HOLDS UP BEAKER WITH
        BLUE LIQUID).

GEORGE APPROACHES JED'S DESK AND TAKES THE BEAKER. AS
HE IS ABOUT TO SIP FROM IT, JED STOPS HIM.

                    JED (CONT'D)
        Oh, sorry, not that beaker. I think
        that's the one with the lethal
        cocktail in it. Here, try this one.
        (HOLDS UP BEAKER WITH RED LIQUID).

                    GEORGE
            (relieved but also worried)
        Are you sure this time?

                    JED
        Am I sure? Of course I'm sure.

GEORGE DRINKS FROM THE BEAKER.

                    JED (CONT'D)
        I think.

TRENT ENTERS AND HANGS UP HIS COAT.

                    TRENT
        Wow, did I have a great dinner.

                    JED
        Where'd you go, boss?

                    TRENT
        I went to that new French place
        that just opened up on the other
        side of town. Boy was it delicious.
        They've got the best chef in the
        whole state.

SALLY LIFTS HER HEAD OFF THE DESK, SQUEALS, THEN DROPS
HER HEAD BACK TO THE DESK.

                    TRENT (CONT'D)
        Oh, I'm sorry Sally. I didn't mean
        anything by that. You're a great
        chef too. Hey, what happened to the
        Food Network people? Weren't they

going to film your last meal?

                    SALLY

They left. Turns out they didn't
really want to film me going to the
McDonald's on Route 75 and buying a
cheeseburger and fries.

                    TRENT

Oh, that's a real shame. Well,
don't get too down. There are
plenty of other death row inmates.
And I doubt the new Governor will
be giving any of them clemency.
She's a real tough cookie that one.
Point is that you'll have plenty of
other chances to make a great final
meal. You just have to be patient.

                    SALLY

Yeah, I guess you're right.

                    TRENT

        (smacking his lips)

Boy, I can still taste that cognac
infused chocolate eclair. Wow.

                    SALLY

Ohhhh.

FATHER MCCONNELL ENTERS, WOBBLING UNSTEADILY.

                    MCCONNELL

OK, where's this prisoner I'm
supposed to counsel?

                    TRENT

Hey there, Father. Nice to see
you. Rusty's back in his cell.
That's where we tend to keep the
prisoners.

                    MCCONNELL

Great. I better get back there.
Don't want anyone spending the rest

of eternity in hell on my watch.

                    GEORGE
So, Father, you have a liquid lunch
today?

                    MCCONNELL
Look, if you had my job, you'd
drink too.

MCCONNELL WALKS BY JED'S DESK ON HIS WAY TO THE
CELLBLOCK. HE SEES THE BLUE BEAKER AND PICKS IT UP.

                MCCONNELL (CONT'D)
Ahh, a Blue Hawaii. Very tropical.

        (he drinks it and leaves)
                    JED
Well, I guess we're going to find
out whether the lethal cocktail
works.

SOUNDS OF LOUD PROTESTORS ARE HEARD OUT THE WINDOW.
THEY ARE CHANTING "DOWN WITH THE WARDEN" OVER AND OVER
AGAIN. TRENT LOOKS OUT THE WINDOW AND SEES STEPHANIE
LEADING THE CHANT.

                    TRENT
        (heading for the door)
All right, that's it. Now it's
personal. I'm going out there.

                                    CUT TO:

                    ACT II

                    SCENE C

EXT. OUTSIDE PRISON – MOMENTS LATER
(STEPHANIE, TRENT, FEMALE PROTESTOR)

TRENT ANGRILY APPROACHES THE CROWD OF PROTESTORS LED
BY STEPHANIE, WHO IS CHANTING "DOWN WITH THE WARDEN."

                    STEPHANIE

Oh, look everyone. Here he is.
Trent Hatfield, the prison warden.

THE CROWD BOOS.

                      TRENT

The Constitution may give you the
right to protest the execution, but
protesting me is going too far. I'm
just doing my job.

                    STEPHANIE

Did you hear that everyone? He's
just doing his job. He's just
carrying out the state's immoral
and inhumane punishment.

THE CROWD BOOS MORE.

                      TRENT

The voters of this state have
overwhelmingly approved of the
death penalty. And I am proud to
be the one who makes sure they get
what they want.

                    STEPHANIE

Oh, sure. Even if it means
occasionally executing an innocent
person or two.

                      TRENT

That's why we have appeals. That's
why it takes fifteen years before
someone is actually executed. All
those people let off death row
because they're innocent just prove
that the system works.

                    STEPHANIE

Can you prove that no innocent
person has been put to death?

                    TRENT

    No. Can you prove that one innocent
    person has been put to death?

                  STEPHANIE

        (frustrated)

    Down with the warden. Down with the
    warden.

THE CROWD TAKES UP THE CHANT.

                    TRENT

    Fine. I see there's no reasoning
    with you. Enjoy wasting the rest of
    your day. I have work to do.

TRENT RETURNS TO THE PRISON. THE CROWD CONTINUES TO
CHANT. A <u>FEMALE PROTESTOR</u> APPROACHES STEPHANIE.

                FEMALE PROTESTOR

    Great job, Stephanie. You really
    showed him, that big dumb meathead.

                  STEPHANIE

    Yeah. He is kind of handsome
    though.

                FEMALE PROTESTOR

    What?

                  STEPHANIE

    Oh, nothing.

                  <u>ACT II</u>

                  <u>SCENE D</u>

<u>INT. CELLLBLOCK - NIGHT</u>
(HARRY, PATRICIA, WINSTON, SALLY, RUSTY, MCCONNELL,
TRENT, JED, GEORGE, GARY)

THE ENTIRE PRISON STAFF IS SITTING AROUND IN THE
CELLBLOCK WAITING FOR A CALL FROM THE SUPREME COURT
ABOUT RUSTY'S FINAL APPEAL. THE CLOCK ON THE WALL
READS 11:45.

HARRY

(leafing through brochures)

Hey, which Hawaiian island do guys
think I should spend Christmas on,
Maui or the big island? I mean,
the big island has those cool
volcanoes, but Maui has the great
beaches.

PATRICIA

What are you talking about? You're
on death row. You'll be lucky if
you get an hour in the exercise
yard for Christmas.

HARRY

Speak for yourself. With my lawyer,
I'll probably be out by Halloween.
Hmm, maybe I should go on an
African safari instead. I've always
wanted to see a giraffe in the
wild.

WINSTON

I'm a giraffe.

SALLY

No you're not.

WINSTON

I'm kind of a giraffe.

RUSTY

(finishing up his
cheeseburger)

Boy, was that delicious.
(BELCHING). Whoa. Does anyone have
an antacid?

SALLY

I guess you're regretting your
choice of a last meal now, huh?

RUSTY

Oh, no. It was worth it. I mean,
my heartburn is only going to
last fifteen minutes anyway. Hey,
Father, are you going to make sure
I'm saved, or what?

MCCONNELL

(groaning)

I'm so constipated.

TRENT

Jed, I really hope you've finally
figured out this lethal cocktail.
It's going to be real embarrassing
if all Rusty gets out of it is a
severe case of gas and bloating.

JED

Don't worry, boss. I just had the
proportions wrong. There is a good
chance that it's going to work
now. You know, we never had these
problems back when we just used
the rack. I mean, sure, sometimes
it took several days for the guy's
body to pull apart into several
pieces, but, hey, them's the
breaks.

EVERYONE GRIMACES. GEORGE LAUGHS.

TRENT

What's with you? What's so funny?

GEORGE

I have no idea. I'm so high. I love
Demoral. (LOOKS AT HIS BURNT UP
HAND). Look, my hand's all burnt
up. Ha, ha.

GARY ENTERS. HE'S VERY EXCITED.

GARY

OK, I just talked to the clerk at
the Supreme Court. They're going to
hand down their decision any minute
now.

TRENT

(approaching the phone on
the wall)

All right. I guess I'll get ready
to answer the phone.

EVERYONE IS QUIET FOR A FEW MOMENTS. EVERYONE IS
ANXIOUSLY WAITING FOR THE PHONE TO RING. A PHONE
RINGS. TRENT ANSWERS THE PHONE ON THE WALL.

TRENT (CONT'D)

Hello? Hello?

THE PHONE KEEPS RINGING.

TRENT (CONT'D)

Hello?

GARY

(realizing the ring is
coming from his cell phone)

Oh, that's me. (ANSWERS HIS PHONE).
Hi, honey. Yes, I should be home
soon. I'm sorry I'm so late.
(PAUSE) I wub you too. (PAUSE) No,
I wub you the best.

EVERYONE GROANS.

GARY (CONT'D)

I've got to go honey. Bye. (HE
HANGS UP). Sorry about that.

MORE ANXIOUS WAITING. THE PHONE ON THE WALL RINGS.
TRENT ANSWERS IT.

TRENT

Hello? Oh, hello there Chief

Justice. You have? You've reached a
decision on Rusty's appeal? Great,
what is it? Oh, wait, can you hold
on? I've got call waiting. (CLICKS
PHONE). Hi. What? Really? A credit
card with no annual fee? And only
23% interest? Sign me up.

EVERYONE GROANS.

> TRENT (CONT'D)

Oh, sorry. Can you call back? I've
got an important call on the other
line. Thanks. (CLICKS PHONE). Hi,
Chief Justice. Sorry about that?
OK, what's the decision? Really?
All right. I'll let everyone know.
Thanks a lot. Good night.

TRENT HANGS UP.

> SALLY

So, what is it?

> TRENT

Well, it turns out I can get a
Discover Card at a low annual rate
and get one hundredth of a percent
cash back on all of my purchases.

> JED

Not that. Rusty's case.

> TRENT

Oh, yeah. Right. The Supreme Court
granted the stay. They sent the
case back to the appellate court to
consider whether it was illegal for
the police to search Rusty's house
without a warrant.

EVERYONE ERUPTS IN APPLAUSE AND CONGRATULATIONS FOR
RUSTY AND GARY.

                    RUSTY

All right. I guess I'm going to be
here when my grandson is born next
month after all.

                    TRENT

Don't get too comfortable, Rusty.
The execution will probably be set
again before you know it.

                    RUSTY

Oh, that's OK. At least I'll
get to eat another McDonald's
cheeseburger.

                    SALLY

No way. I've got a few months now
to convince you to let me cook you
a delicious last meal.

                    RUSTY

All right, I guess I'll let you try
to convince me. No promises though.

                    SALLY

I better give the guys at the Food
Network a call and let them know
the special is back on.

                    JED

And I have a little extra time to
make sure I've got the formula for
the lethal cocktail right.

JED HOLDS UP A BEAKER FILLED WITH A GOLD BUBBLING
LIQUID. FATHER MCCONNELL EYES IT ENTHUSIASTICALLY.

                    MCCONNELL

Mmm, champagne. I'll drink to that.

HE DRINKS FROM THE BEAKER, GROANS, AND COLLAPSES.
GEORGE CACKLES MANIACALLY.

TAG

<u>INT. INSIDE OF OLD SPARKY'S BAR - ABOUT 1 O'CLOCK A.M.</u>
(TRENT, SALLY, JED, GEORGE, STEPHANIE)

OLD SPARKY'S BAR IS THE NEIGHBORHOOD WATERING HOLE
WHERE THE PRISON STAFF HANGS OUT AFTER WORK. A NEON
ELECTRIC CHAIR SIZZLES ON AND OFF BEHIND THE BAR.
GEORGE, JED, SALLY, AND TRENT ARE AT THE BAR DRINKING.

TRENT

Well, it looks like Father
McConnell is going to be all right.

SALLY

Yeah, the doctor said he just needs
a good strong enema and a little
rest, and he'll be good as new.

JED

I guess it was a good thing Rusty's
execution didn't go forward. That
would have been embarrassing. I
wonder what the problem was. Maybe
too much food coloring? You know it
didn't used to be this hard.

GEORGE

Yeah, yeah. It was so much easier
back when you just threw stones
at the criminal. We know, we know
already.

JED

Well, it was easier.

STEPHANIE ENTERS THE BAR AND TAKES A SEAT NEXT TO
TRENT. SHE GETS THE BARTENDER'S ATTENTION.

STEPHANIE

Hi. I'll have a bourbon, straight
up.

TRENT NOTICES STEPHANIE.

TRENT

Oh, you. Great. I bet you're pretty
happy tonight with the stay and
all. I guess you're celebrating,
huh?

STEPHANIE

(downing her drink)

No, I'm not happy. I mean, I'm
happy that Rusty didn't get
executed tonight, but I'm not
happy that we still have the death
penalty and that hundreds of people
are going to be executed this year
in the United States.

TRENT

I don't get it. What's the big
deal? Look, it's an eye for an
eye. You've got to meet killing
with killing. How else can there be
justice?

STEPHANIE

Even if that was right, our system
is so flawed that it can't be just.
I mean, all the studies show that
the death penalty is carried out in
a racially discriminatory manner
and that defendants don't get
trained lawyers.

TRENT

I know the system's not completely
perfect, but no system of justice
ever is.

STEPHANIE

Well, are you proud that the United
States executes more people per
year than every country other than
China and Iran?

TRENT

(takes a drink and considers

(the question)

No, not particularly. But what
about you? Are you against the
death penalty in all cases? What
about Timothy McVeigh? He killed
over 200 people, many of them
children. Do you think he didn't
deserve the death penalty?

STEPHANIE

(pauses to consider the
question)

Well, I don't know. Maybe he's
different.

EVERYONE AT THE BAR IS QUIET, THINKING ABOUT THE DEATH
PENALTY. SUDDENLY, TRENT AND STEPHANIE SPEAK TO THE
BARTENDER AT THE SAME TIME.

TRENT

Bartender. Another drink. And make
it a double.

STEPHANIE

(at the same time as Trent)

Bartender. Another drink. And make
it a double.

FADE OUT.

In the Trunk

Garvey turns on his side to relieve the pain in his back. The tire iron is blunt and best avoided as much as possible. He pats the worn carpet with his right hand, grabs hold of the small bottle of who knows what with his left. The smell of fried clams is overwhelming. Perhaps the coast is near. But there are many coasts, and these days clams can be shipped anywhere. Who knows, maybe they are in a Red Lobster parking lot on the outskirts of Kansas City. It is probably hopeless. Should he drink from the mystery bottle? What kind of roulette would that be? Irish? He decides: No, he'll wait this out, see what happens.

I can't catch my breath because the mountain is too steep. The air in Azerbaijan this morning is crisp and pleasant as usual, but my lungs are weak, the shame has withered them beyond their years. Why I would climb in this condition is a topic of much gossip in the village. The old women tease me and poke me with sharp sticks before they serve me the mutton dish I love so much. Across the precipice I spot the endangered leopard and choose to climb in the opposite direction. I am confident that this choice, at least, I won't regret come nightfall.

At a lower elevation now, I regain my breath. I sit on a sandy rock fishing for dinner sturgeon and am reminded of a scene from years past. Me and Garvey, in the old neighborhood, spear fishing for mackerel in one of Minnesota's thousand blue pools, working out the details for a commercial venture now gone terribly wrong. Garvey is the ideas man, I run the numbers. Looking back now, as the wind off the steppe blows mountain grasses into my unruly mane, it seems obvious that nobody was ever going to buy what we had to offer. Who, after all, really needs a set of "anti-asteroid" armor anyway?

In the trunk, Garvey listens intently to the sounds outside, tries to discern where they might be located. He hears some busy chattering, what sounds like argumentation, but the details are drowned out by a pulsating beat and the chirping of some annoying boy band. He had figured that by now, after all these days, his eyes would have somehow adjusted to the darkness of his tiny cavern, but that isn't the case. He knows exactly where his quickly depleting store of Saltines brand snack crackers is hidden, but other than that he is lost, lost in the smallest possible place one could ever be lost.

Frisco issued his proposal, we were split on its merits. He was from the wrong part of town, it is true, but we were at the end of our ropes, our warehouses filled with dusty unused metal suits, bank accounts sinking alongside our hopes. My eyes were filled with rubies, I was discombobulated with greed. Garvey raised objections, issued protests, urged persistence in our existing enterprise. In the end I prevailed, citing endless ludicrous pie-in-the-skies: high definition plasmatic flat screens, his and hers hybrid fueled Jaguars, significant (albeit minority) interests in a Minneapolis Arena Football expansion franchise. I realize now that I should have been careful with my gifts. Garvey spent high school twiddling beakers in the science club; I gave myself to debate. Words, rhetoric, argumentation: these are my weapons, but I should have been more careful with them. I certainly should not have used them in the name of gems.

The day of the heist not a thing went right. My shower lasted too long, Frisco forgot the keys, nobody wore a watch. Alarms were tripped, fingerprints left. The papers spoke of something called "felony murder," but I can't say I ever really understood the concept. We escaped but just barely. A precinct was devoted to our capture, overtime hours were logged, acquaintances interrogated. We knew they wanted Frisco, would go through us to get him, and Frisco knew it too. Orders were communicated in back alleys, through untrustworthy couriers. Leave, leave the country. Go far, do not return. For me little persuasion was necessary, as I've long felt the urge to walk the central Asian plains. For Garvey, though, it was not so easy. At the greasy spoon in our final stolen minutes together, backs firmly planted against the wall, he spoke of family, though he was childless, and dreams of graduate work, though his undergraduate record was spotty. For once my gift failed me; I quickly grabbed the next charter to Baku, and as my DC-10 descended over the Caspian Sea, I realized that Garvey and I had met for the last time.

The village leader approaches me, and we resume our ongoing negotiations. He will cut me in on his illicit caviar trade if I will use my contacts to get him statin drugs. Ever since the Red Cross volunteer tested his LDL cholesterol three months ago, the leader has feared not only a painful early death but also his village's fate if his delinquent idiot of a first born son is left in charge. I have debated the pros and cons of this arrangement end-lessly. Of course I should learn from my past mistakes, but biology is hard to shake, and I think I already know how this story will end.

The car lurches forward and picks up speed. Garvey wakes with a start and inhales deeply. The salt is heavy in the air here, he realizes—they are definitely near the sea. What Garvey does not know is that he is presently the car's only occupant, and that the sea he smells is the ocean on the other side of the quickly approaching cliff.

Sorry, Garv.

Methodology

At seven-thirty in the morning on Monday, July the sixteenth, Larry awoke to a single, shrill cackle emanating from inside the vaporizer that sat at the end of his bed. It was the sixteenth day in a row that he had woken up in this fashion. Though a natural curiosity and rising frustration level tempted him to open the vaporizer to discover what hidden entity was cackling at him each morning, his naked fear held him back from carrying out this plan. Larry was afraid of many things. One of these things was the prospect of opening up his vaporizer to find a severe-looking bird-like creature with fiery yellow eyes, a razor sharp red beak, and oily olive green scales which would leap out and kill him painfully by tearing out a vital body part. This he did not need, and so, as he had done all month, Larry ignored the vaporizer, scratched his belly, and got ready for work.

The first person Larry saw at the law library where he had labored for the past eight months was Theodore, his impeccably dressed boss. Today Theodore was wearing a deep blue Armani suit with a perfectly matched tie. Larry had always been jealous of his boss's flawless sense of fashion, but he had no inkling that in fact Theodore was a lowly level fourteen alien lifeform from Discon, a class M planet in the Beta Galaxy, who only dressed well in order to fool his coworkers into thinking that he was actually an earthling.

"Well, well, Larry," Theodore said in greeting. "You look a little wan this morning. Too much carousing last night, I presume? No matter. I'm certain your indefatigable *joie de vivre* will propel you through another day of monotonous shelving and reshelving at our esteemed *bibliotechque*. What do you say, my good man?"

"Yes, I think so," Larry answered timidly, unaware that Theodore's use of pompous British diction and French multi-syllabic words were simply additional ploys to fool his friends and colleagues.

"Good. Glad to hear it. You can begin by organizing the dusty tomes on old English Admiralty Law, and when you're finished with those volumes, why don't you start in on the commentaries on the commentaries on Blackstone's Commentaries. You'll find them all stacked in the QQ section down in basement level three. Have fun!" Theodore turned on his polished penny loafers and returned to the reference room where he often practiced his counting of digits.

Down in basement level three, Larry surveyed the ancient, decrepit Admiralty Law section and sat down at a nearby carrel. He placed his hands over his face in despair and moaned. Oh why oh why did he let his relationship with Trudy end? He knew that he should not have allowed her to accept the stuffed toy that C.W. Wim, the milkman, had given her for Tu Bishvat. He knew that he should not have let him accompany her to that lecture on maple trees that the local botanist offered at the town library. He knew he should not have let him carry her away while he sat helplessly at the kitchen table eating a sandwich. Larry imagined them as they must be now, grinning stupidly over some joke about bark, trading furtive glances over an acorn—Oh, God!—how could he have ever let her be stolen away from him by a milkman turned amateur dendrologist?

"And, goddammit!" he suddenly yelled to the speechless shelves of books around him, "What the fuck is living in my vaporizer?"

At this utterance, a man dressed in a tan corduroy suit appeared from behind a stack of books and limped slowly towards Larry. The man was quite short, as though a lack of dairy products in his early teens had stunted his growth. His closely-shaven head was wide and flat; Larry's first thought at the sight of him was that he could probably serve a candlelight dinner for two on top of it. The man's chocolate brown eyes were the exact color of the square, knitted tie that hung around his neck. His pants quit about two inches above his navy blue, worn-out New Balance sneakers to reveal two red-striped tube socks that had flopped down about his hairy ankles. Larry was quite impressed.

"Hello," the man said. "I am Zatwig."

"Hi. Good to meet you. I'm Larry."

The two men shook hands. From the warm, peaty sweat exuding from Zatwig's palm, Larry knew that he had met a trustworthy man, a man as solid and reliable as the planet Jupiter.

"I'm sorry if my screaming interrupted your work," Larry said.

"Oh, no. You did not interrupt my work," Zatwig said. "I do not have any work."

"Then what do you do in the basement of the law library, Zatwig?"

"I wait for people like you, Larry," Zatwig said sparkly. "It seems you have some kind of problem with your vaporizer, and I would like to help you with it."

Larry's face suddenly beamed with delight like an ant that has just been fried by some juvenile delinquent's magnifying glass. "Oh, I think you just may be able to," he said, suppressing a giggle. He sat down and explained the problems that had been plaguing him for the last sixteen days—the shrill cackle, the timid indecision, the incessant curiosity. When he was through, Zatwig, who was standing on top of a British Admiralty Law treatise published in 1889, scratched his head with his long, crusty fingernails and announced: "Larry, let us return to the apartment and work ourselves out of this ball of skin, shall we?"

At his apartment on the second floor of a dilapidated building on the corner of Birch and Madison, Zatwig offered Larry a steaming cup of hot white chocolate. Though it was a brutally hot day and the apartment was filled with flying insects, Larry sucked down the hot liquid with gusto.

"Love your hot white chocolate," Larry said, wiping the sweat off his upper lip with a stained cleanex and swatting at a wasp that had landed on the edge of his grimy cup. Zatwig placed a tray of petit fours on the coffee table and sat down.

"I love what you've done with the petit fours," Larry said, holding a petit four up to the fluorescent light and admiring its pink frosting.

"Ehhh, could you please just give it a rest," Zatwig blurted.

"Oh. Yeah. Right. Sorry," Larry mumbled. "So, what do you think about my vaporizer?"

"Well," Zatwig began, concentrating initially on a hangnail that had sprouted from his thumb. "Of course we'll need to choose a methodology."

"Of course," Larry answered. "Can't go far without a methodology."

"The question is *which* methodology!" Zatwig plucked his hangnail off his thumb. A tiny drop of red blood spilled out and plopped into the white chocolate, where it spread out like a bad rumor.

"Naturally," said Larry. "Can't go around using just any old methodology. In fact, I've already considered a number of methodologies myself, but in terms of finding the best methodology I'm unsure whether or not...."

"Oh, Christ! Will you please shut the fuck up!?" Zatwig shouted, clearing the table of hot chocolate, petit fours and wasps with a single swipe of his fat hand. "Just *shut up* already!"

"I'm sorry," said Larry. "I didn't mean it."

Zatwig sighed. "As I was saying, we must think carefully if we want to solve the vaporizer problem. We cannot be shouting our mouths off about methods if we don't even know what *method* we want to employ."

Larry nodded his enthusiastic assent, and Zatwig stood up from his chair, hoisting his pants up to the bottom of his rib cage. Larry caught a glance of Zatwig's hairy legs peeping up at him over the stripes in the tube socks, and he smiled deliciously at this unexpected surprise.

Zatwig walked deliberately into his bedroom and returned moments later with a large volume entitled "Methodology." He sat back down in his chair and began leafing through the pages, muttering softly to himself.

"Mmmm. Yes. Uh huh. Well, maybe. Ah hah! No, no." Zatwig proceeded in this fashion for what seemed to Larry to be a very long time and then closed the book with a thud not unlike the thud one might hear at the closing of a large chemistry, or econometrics book, or some other large book.

"I understand completely now," Zatwig exclaimed. "All told there are only eight possible methodologies that could even begin to solve your vaporizer problem. Of these, all but Method A and Method D are completely inappropriate. Of the remaining two methods, D may seem like it could work. Don't get me wrong—superficially, Method D seems very reasonable. However, on closer inspection we find that Method D is not only infeasible but it also will most likely result in the reverse of the result you were expecting. On top of all this, Method D is more Mumfordian than anything else."

"Ahh," nodded Larry. "I see."

"I suggest very strongly, Larry," Zatwig said, standing up and hiking his shirt up to his nipples, "that you implement Method A to solve your problem. I want you to give this some thought and return here Wednesday with your decision. That will be all." Zatwig offered his hand and Larry shook it, feeling immeasurably better than he had ever since his vaporizer had began cackling over a fortnight ago. He took a last petit four up from off the filthy floor where it was swimming in a puddle of dusty hot white chocolate and headed for the door.

Shirtless, hatless and mucking around in a pile of his own mental excrement, Mumford approached Larry while the latter was slurping mouthfuls of water from a fountain which stood in the middle of Larry's favorite park.

"You Zatwig lover, you," Mumford said sharply, causing Larry to choke and inhale a mouthful of the water up through his nose.

Ashamed at being recognized in the middle of his favorite park, Larry spun around and held out the now squashed petit four.

"Petit four?" he asked.

"Get that shit out of my face," Mumford yelled, slapping the flattened little cake out of Larry's hand and into the fountain, where it floated like a dead puppy. "I'm serious."

"Oh. I'm uhhh, sorry about that," Larry said.

Mumford was dressed only in a pair of tattered, over-sized, grand-maesque panties and Larry had to admit that he was not dressed very well. Nevertheless, Larry admired the way that the waistband of Mumford's panties seemed to be looking up and mocking the bushy tuff of black, curly hair blossoming from Mumford's cavernous bellybutton. Though Mumford's face was a very pale shade of white, he nevertheless sported a 1976 Julius Irving style afro, the greased up curls of which crept down to his forehead to tickle the tips of the creamy whiteheads that sprouted from his slippery red skin. Mumford's hairless chest was also covered with a plethora of juicy pustules which every so often would spontaneously erupt, causing a frothy stream of goo to pour down his fat belly where it would get trapped in those wiry threads that danced tenderly above Mumford's tasty waistband.

"You Zatwig lover, you," Mumford repeated.

Larry was confused. "I enjoy Zatwig—uhh, if that's what you mean. He's a pleasant man and one of great warmth," Larry said defensively.

"Do you deny that you were just in Zatwig's apartment discussing various methodologies?" Mumford asked, raising his voice like a journalist, who, not satisfied with a politician's answer to his first question, raises a follow-up inquiry.

"I don't deny the accusation, though I'm not sure I see why my being in Zatwig's apartment should upset you so much."

"You stinkin' Zatwig lover," Mumford reiterated.

"Ohh...," Larry said, experiencing a sudden burst of insight. "You must be Mumford."

"Well, welcome to the big top, naaasty maaan," Mumford replied, jamming his fist down the front of his panties. "Who the hell else could I have been?"

"Yeah," agreed Larry. "Who else?"

"Look, I don't want to upset you, Larry," Mumford said, putting his hand on top of Larry's head, "and I can see that you feel bad right now because I said all that stuff about your being a Zatwig lover and everything, but all I want you to do is consider Method D as a possible solution to your vaporizer problem. Is that too much to ask?" Mumford pulled out a crinkly old brochure entitled "Method D" from his panties and handed it to Larry, who accepted it with glee.

"Wow, thanks," he said.

"Method D, as you will discover from reading the literature, is a fool-proof method for solving your problem. Method A, on the other hand, is about as good of a method as eating a thimble full of strained eggplant to cure an advanced case of diphtheria. You wouldn't eat a thimble full of strained eggplant to cure an advanced case of diphtheria, now would you, Larry?"

"I don't even like eggplant," Larry answered.

"Then there you go. Quid est demonstratum, my friend."

"Ahhh, yes," said Larry. "The ol' QED."

"Good. I'll meet you in Zatwig's living room at twelve o'clock noon on Wednesday to discuss your decision concerning the methodology. And remember, Larry," Mumford said gravely, "the decision is yours and yours alone." Mumford then removed his hand from Larry's head, turned around and sprinted wildly away from Larry, waving his hands in the air like a maniac and singing "Skip, skip, skip to my loo," in a preening falsetto voice until Larry could no longer see his greasy curls fluttering above the receding horizon.

Larry, astounded at the incredible luck he had suddenly encountered, put the brochure in his back pocket and returned home to do some serious thinking.

Tuesday passed like a pair of pliers. On Wednesday morning Larry awoke for the eighteenth day in a row to a single shrill cackle emanating from inside the vaporizer that sat at the end of his bed. This time, however, Larry was not afraid. He had spent the last thirty-six hours carefully mulling over Method A and Method D, and he had finally come to a conclusion that would solve his vaporizer problem once and for all. After making comprehensive lists of each method's pros and cons, weighing these advantages and disadvantages against each other, and asking himself what Trudy would do in such a situation, Larry decisively decided to let Mumford and Zatwig decide for him. He was very pleased with himself for coming to such a cunning conclusion, and he taunted the vaporizer mercilessly, his new decision affording him a sense of self-confidence not possessed since before Trudy's abrupt departure on the arm of that awful milkman.

"Stupid thing! Stupid thing!" Larry taunted, dancing and twirling about the vaporizer with delight. "You're a really stupid thing!"

"Cackle, cackle," the thing responded.

"Ya dumb dipshit!" Larry sang. "You shitty dipshit!"

"Cackle cackle."

At the library, Larry shelved books with gusto, checking his watch constantly in eager anticipation of 11:45, when he would sneak out the back exit and go to Zatwig's house to announce his decision regarding the methodology to Zatwig and Mumford. He was so happy that he almost threw up several times, but each time was able to swallow the saucy bile before it spurted out and soiled the violet ascot that he had deliberately donned for this very important day.

When it was 11:45, Larry snuck by Theodore's office, where Theodore was inexplicably saying the alphabet to himself very slowly, and rushed out into the midday heat.

Standing in Zatwig's doorstep, Larry felt as excited as a little kid who had just received a better-than-average report card. He knocked on Zatwig's door and waited for it to open. When it did, Larry was greeted by a very angry Zatwig.

"I'm mad at you," Zatwig said sternly. "Now get in here."

Larry felt a little deflated that Zatwig would be upset with him, but he figured that it was probably just nerves. He entered the apartment, still feeling the sweet tingle of happiness quivering in his mercury-filled teeth. He sat down in a seat directly across from Mumford, who, still wearing nothing but his flimsy panties, was speaking with a hornet that had landed on his wrist.

"Hello, little hornet," Mumford said.

"Hi, Mumford," said Larry.

Mumford ignored Larry and kept talking to the hornet.

Before long, Zatwig entered the room with his volume on methodology and sat down in an empty chair.

"No hot white chocolate this time, Zatwig?" Larry asked in a giddy voice.

"You stupid motherfucker!" Zatwig cursed.

"Oh, gosh," uttered Larry. "This isn't going at all the way I thought it would."

Zatwig took a deep breath and regained his composure. Then he spoke slowly, with his characteristically perfect diction and enunciation. "Well," he said. "I didn't think it would come to this. I mean, I didn't think that we'd have to deal with any *Mumfordian* nonsense. I *thought* that we had decided to employ Method A, but since it seems that this is not necessarily the case and that Method D has now somehow made an appearance in your paltry little thought processes, I guess you better inform us of your decision, Larry. You have made a decision, haven't you?"

"Oh, yes, I have," Larry said, bursting with joy.

"Well, let's have it," said Zatwig.

Larry looked over at Mumford, who was still staring down at his hornet, looking like a defendant about to hear his verdict. He then looked back at Zatwig and flashed a silly grin. "The decision is... I've decided to let you two decide between yourselves."

A pause.

"Of course you realize, you idiot," Zatwig said softly, "that Mumford and I are *enemies!*"

"Oh? Really?" Larry asked, crestfallen. He looked at Mumford for support, but in Zatwig's presence, Mumford seemed an entirely different man from the one he had so admired in the park.

"It's true. You're a real shit for brains, Larry," Mumford muttered.

Larry considered the situation silently for a few moments. "I have an idea," he suddenly said, springing to life once again. "Even though you two are enemies, you can still decide which method I should use."

Zatwig was exasperated. He tried to explain as logically as possible why Larry's suggestion was impossible. "No, Larry, we can't do that because, you see, we both think our own method is right and the other's method is wrong. Moreover, Mumford and I hate each other's guts and neither of us would ever decide to recommend the other's method."

Larry felt sad. He looked over at Mumford again with pleading eyes, but Mumford simply nodded. "Well," whined Larry, "can't you guys just decide?"

"You fuckbag!" Zatwig screamed, throwing the methodology book at Larry's head, barely missing it. "Get out! Get out! Get out of my house!"

Scared and dumbfounded, Larry stood up and scurried out the door.

"Method D is an excellent method," Mumford called out to Larry, who was running down the stairs.

"You shut up," bellowed Zatwig.

The next two days were very difficult for Larry, who, following the inexplicable happenings at Zatwig's house, had fallen into an uncomfortable funk. He did not show up for work at the library on either Thursday or Friday, feeling too jostled by recent failures to be able to reshelve even a single small book. He knew that he was ensuring his swift dismissal from his job—Theodore was too smart and down to earth to let him get away with such behavior—but he didn't much care. He just sat all day long in his rocking chair and sniffled, once in a while getting up to go to the washroom, where he would retrieve a tissue and wipe the drippy snot from off of his chin.

On Saturday, after waking up for the twenty-first time to the sound of a single shrill cackle emanating from inside the vaporizer that sat at the end of his bed, Larry went back to his favorite park. He sat down on his favorite bench and sighed. "Oh," he complained, "if only I had not let Trudy go off with C.W. Wim! If only I had been able to get a better job! If only I had chosen the right methodology!"

Suddenly, Larry heard a sound coming from behind him. "Pssssst... Larry... Over here," he heard. He turned around to see Mumford attempting to hide his fat frame behind a twig that he was holding in his left hand.

"Mumford!" Larry said enthusiastically. "What are you doing wearing that three piece Brooks Brothers Suit?"

"Shhhhh," Mumford said, putting his index finger in his ear. "Zatwig doesn't know I'm here."

"Oh," Larry responded with a whisper. "I'm sorry. I wasn't aware of that fact."

Larry tiptoed over to Mumford's twig, careful not to make even the slightest bit of noise that might alert Zatwig, who was dozing fitfully in his apartment two miles away, to their meeting. At the twig, the two men shook hands.

"Hey!" Larry said. "Great cuff links."

"Thanks. I picked them out from a Service Merchandise catalog."

"Wow. So, what's going on?"

"I just wanted to come and tell you that you don't have to listen to Zatwig. You do not have to be a Zatwig lover."

Larry was stunned. "I don't?"

"No. In fact, you can go ahead and employ Method D without ever consulting Zatwig. If you want, you can be completely Zatwig-free."

"Really? You mean that I could just listen to you? I could just use your method?"

"Exactly, my brave and dear Larry. I implore you to employ Method D to solve your vaporizer problem and emancipate yourself from the airtight grip of Zatwig."

Larry was overcome with a fresh wave of ecstasy. In a flash of sudden realization, abetted by the wise words of this pimply, well-dressed Mumford, Larry had realized what he should have realized all long. That he didn't need Zatwig. That he could be Zatwigless and still save his own poor self from destruction. Who was this Zatwig, anyway? Just some table-headed jerk with a bad temper. Why had he felt that Zatwig held the answer to the vaporizer problem when Mumford—yes, Mumford!—had known the proper method to solve the vaporizer problem? Oh, Jesus Up Above In Heaven, what a man this Mumford was.

Larry told Mumford that he would most certainly employ Method D.

"Yeah, great," Mumford said. "Just make sure you don't let Zatwig know I was here, O.K.?"

"Uhh, why not?" Larry asked, confused.

"Because I think he would be very mad," Mumford replied.

"Oh, yeah. We don't want him to be very mad at us," Larry replied.

"Thanks, Larry. And good luck," Mumford said solemnly. He then threw down his twig, dropped to his knees and somersaulted repeatedly until he was out of Larry's eyesight.

Larry plunged his fist into the air and began jogging home, thinking all the way about how terrific it was going to be to employ Method D.

It was only after he had laid out all of the necessary materials for implementing Method D and had completely psyched himself up for the procedure that Larry suddenly decided that he had better inform Zatwig of his plans.

Licking a fudgsicle like a jaguar lapping the remains of a freshly killed shrew, Larry strode over to Zatwig's apartment, his heart full of promise and the hope that Zatwig would approve of his plan to employ Method D. When he came to the stairs leading up to Zatwig's apartment, Larry swallowed the last bit of the fudgsicle, put the stick in his pocket and bounded up the staircase.

Unexpectedly, the door to Zatwig's apartment was ajar.

Larry knocked on the door and called out to Zatwig. When there was no response, he entered the apartment gingerly, looking around for any sign of Zatwig. Larry heard the faint sound of a man singing "A Trisket a Trasket a Green and Yellow Basket" coming from the back hallway, and he walked slowly in that direction.

"Oh, Zatwig." Larry called out. "It's Larry. I've come to talk about methodology with you. Oh, Zzzzzzatwig, I've got some issssssues to discuss with you!"

The singing became louder and clearer as Larry made his way down the hallway. When he came to the end of the hall, Larry realized that the singing was coming from behind another closed door. Larry knocked on the door.

"Zatwig? Are you in there? It's Larry."

"Larry?" Zatwig's voice boomed. "Come on in. I'm just taking a little bath."

Larry pushed the door open and nearly fainted when he looked inside. The entire bathroom was splattered with blood from floor to ceiling. Mumford's oily and hairy head, previously attached to Mumford's body, was sitting askew in the blood soaked sink. Zatwig, naked and just a little fat, was splashing about in the blood-filled bathtub and playing with what appeared to be Mumford's liver. The rest of Mumford was splayed about the bathroom in various chunks and slices, but Zatwig looked happier than Larry had ever seen him before.

"My goodness," said Larry. "What have you done with Mumford?"

Zatwig smiled hideously. "Mumford went behind my back," he said, "so now I'm using his hand to *scratch* my back! Ah, ha, ha, ha!!!" Zatwig hoisted Mumford's detached, rigor-mortisized arm from out of the bloodbath and used its rigid claws to scratch his itchy shoulders. "Hey, look up!" he said, lobbing Mumford's liver to Larry, who, caught off guard, unconsciously lifted his hands and caught it.

"Ahhh! A liver! It's a liver! It's a liver!" Larry screamed, throwing the liver back at Zatwig and running as quickly as he could out of Zatwig's apartment and down to the street, hearing Zatwig's wild laughter persisting in the distance.

As he ran home, panting and sweating like he had never panted or sweated before, Zatwig determined definitively that he had no chance but to discard both Method A and Method D and confront the thing in the vaporizer using his own personal method. He knew that the only thing which could save him now was to pull the top off of that vaporizer and deal with the damned thing directly, on its own terms, without any Mumfords or Zatwigs to cloud his judgment. He got to his house, his armpits like a rainforest at high noon, and pushed open the front door, not bothering to close it behind him. Without washing his hands of the blood that stained them, he rushed over to the vaporizer, now cackling frantically, and got ready to pull off its cover to meet his destiny.

"Prepare to die!" Larry screamed at the top of his lungs, and then with a single swipe he ripped the cover off of the vaporizer to find a severe-looking bird-like creature with fiery yellow eyes, a razor sharp red beak, and oily olive green scales which leapt out and killed him painfully by tearing out his tongue, which had been dangling drippily out of his mouth in astonishment at the fulfillment of his most unspeakable fear.

E=mc³

What about it, Dalton, I ask, but he's busy chomping turnips and doesn't appear to hear me. Chrysanthemum is sitting next to him pinching his cheeks. My jowls are not toys, he tells her, and she reluctantly desists. The appetizers have arrived; it's anyone's ball game from here. I examine the soup bowl, am nearly certain that its diameter exceeds two times π times its radius. Removing the string ruler from my neck, I take the relevant measurements, confirm my suspicions. Who says the rules governing the universe are static, I ask my earth-fruit munching chum once again to identical silence. Dalton always orders the "Tuber of the Day" when we come to The Grille because, as he says, it makes him feel at ease with his own corporality and what not. This is fallacy, canards on a stick, a martini of idiocy, shaken not stirred, but Dalton's paying so I let it go. In between the soup course and the main dish, I observe (among other things) the following:

$F = ma$ *plus one.*

$v = v_0 + at$ *divided by 1.0000000000000000001*

$\tau = rF \sin \theta$ *and a smidge*

Chrysanthemum dives into her Ricola®-glazed ham steak, flosses after every bite, tickles Dalton's obliques to his extraordinary dismay. It is clear that Chrysanthemum is in love with Dalton, but I can't really say whether the love is requited. I try to remember the precise order of the Canadian provinces, west to east, while the waiter grinds fresh fish into the water tumblers. There is a fly in my 1982 Chateau Margaux, Dalton suddenly exclaims, and the waiter is over in a flash to disagree. I calculate the velocity of his arrival, am disappointed to find it consistent with prevailing theories. Is it Alberta, then Saskatchewan, or what the Christ is it? For years I've been challenging this whole notion of Avogadro's number; they say it is a constant, defines the number of items in a mole, but in my opinion this has only been established definitively for tiny objects like atoms and paramecia and remains unproven with regard to larger mushy items like marshmallows or scallops or throw pillows. I'd have had this sewn up by now, my research documented in all the leading academic journals, but my grant money dried out years ago so it's all speculation at this point. The waiter is inexplicably wearing a yellow snakeskin ascot that makes him appear like a Liza Minnelli hologram on a Tanzanian safari expedition. Now why the hell would he do that?

Dalton stands and raises his voice, insists that a fly was in his bottle. The waiter fingers his ascot nervously, says no, such a thing is impossible. Dalton responds by plucking the dead fly out of the glass and waving it around like a French flag on Bastille Day; the insect is as big as a small hummingbird but far less delightful. Summoned by the waiter, the sommelier rejects Dalton's position outright, indicates the integrity of the cork, accuses his customer of planting the fly. I whip out my abacus and attempt to calculate certain parameters of permeability but my computations require some data regarding cork density that are available only from the Chateau itself, and there just isn't time. Chrysanthemum is on her knees trying to hold Dalton back as the latter lunges toward the sommelier with his tuber fork in retaliation for the accusation; Dalton makes eight figures so there is little reason for him to plant the fly, and he's a hothead by nature who doesn't take kindly to such finger pointing.

The "experts" say that kinetic energy can be measured by something that looks kind of like

$$KE = \tfrac{1}{2}\,mv^2$$

but my best estimate of Dalton's kinetic energy at this point, as he leaps toward the waiter's throat, tuber fork extended, even incorporating the opposing force exercised by Chrysanthemum as she grabs Dalton's considerable thighs and begs, pleads, beseeches him to stop, is something more like

$$KE = \tfrac{1}{2}\,mv^2, \text{\textit{ or so, give or take two shakes of a tail or what have you}}$$

The waiter intercepts Dalton's attack, grabs the fork away from my friend's clenched digits, lances the substantial fly on the fork's prongs, threatens to feed Dalton the insect with force. Dalton may be rich, but he hasn't taken a shower in days, and the smell of cilantro emanating from his armpits is damned near overpowering. The sommelier is assisting the waiter, and Dalton now finds himself pinned under both of their buttock sets. I take a sip of the fish water and try to remember where Manitoba falls on the west-east Canadian spectrum. Before Saskatchewan? After? As the fly-speared fork prongs slowly descend towards Dalton's sweaty mug, and the sommelier's purple tinged fingers work diligently to part his tightly pressed lips, Chrysanthemum flogs the waiter with her herbed ham steak and implores him at the top of her lungs to leave Dalton alone. Like a maniac she insists that *the wine had a fly, the wine had a fly.* Looking carefully at her for the first time this evening, her hair de-bunned, saliva bubbling from her mouth like one of Old Faithful's smaller neighbors, the sound coming out of her throat reminiscent of an early 80s horror movie victim, I can think of only one thing, and that is this: *I work for an odd financial services firm.* Taking my ruler in hand, I measure the salt shakers, hope for the best.

Horn Incident Report

This room is ridiculously hot, and the walls are closing in. It's like a goddamned coffin in here. This fat guy who calls himself Lugo is stuffed behind a tiny wooden desk pushing buttons on the phone in what seems to be a completely random manner. Every time he hits a button, he says "beep" in a screechy high voice like a helium-inhaling palace concubine. "Beep, beep," he says, pushing the three and the nine. "Beepedy beepedy beep," he squawks.

I'm frustrated as hell, so I try to get Lugo to focus on the task at hand. He's auditing me, and I don't want to spend one more second here than I have to. "Hey, Lugo," I say, "can we get back to the June 15th report, or what?"

Lugo turns abruptly towards me and pulls his lumpy fingers off the phone. I've startled him, broken his concentration. "Beep?" he says.

"June 15th, Lardass," I say. I know it's not the best strategy in the world—ridiculing the county official who is responsible for determining whether I've complied with the federal Horn Honking Reduction Act of 2003 by filling out a Horn Incident Report with the Central Office each time I engage the horn on my aging 1992 Honda Civic LX. But after spending the last ten hours in this sweatbox, my patience, as they say, is wearing thin.

"Oh, yeah, right," Lugo says, opening up a manila folder from the desk and shuffling through the various reports and papers inside. This guy is downright physically difficult to look at. Fleshy jowls resembling a horse's scrotum droop from his chin. Sweat beads well up on the top of his bald head and occasionally trickle down to settle in his hairy ear holes. And ever since he inexplicably removed his shirt about seven hours ago, I've been unable to take my eyes off of the dark purplish mushroom that appears to be growing in the dank, moist space between the fourth and fifth fat roll on the left side of his outrageously large stomach.

"It says here on the printout that you engaged your horn three consecutive times at approximately 5:30 p.m. on June the 15th, but we have no Horn Incident Report on file with respect to that incident. Can you explain yourself?"

I can barely bring myself to open my mouth. It's been like this all day. Sure, I understand what motivated the Congress to promulgate the statute. Noise pollution was rampant, the public was up in arms. Representative Jones drafted the legislation on his antique Smith and Corona, and the fans went wild. A filibuster was instigated, but the Gentleman from Oklahoma raised a point of parliamentary procedure and was promptly impeached. Acting on behalf of her constituents, the Majority Whip insisted on doing the Macarena while the Special Interests called the vote to cloture. Logrolling ensued, and so of course the Speaker exercised his pocket veto, heh, heh, heh, if you know what I mean.

"Look, Lugo," I say, unable to avoid being difficult. "I have no idea what you're talking about. Either I didn't engage the horn or I did file a report. How do I know which one we're dealing with?"

A bead of sweat forms on Lugo's upper lip. "Farber, we have gone over this perhaps five hundred times already today," he says. "The Horn Engagement Device that you installed in your Civic LX to meet the requirements of the statute automatically informs us through state-of-the-art wireless technology every time you engage your horn. The law then requires you to fill out a Horn Incident Report, in triplicate, within thirty days of the engagement, explaining your reason for horn engagement as well as your reflections upon whether, in hindsight, your horn engagement was justified. The legislature made the reasonable determination that such requirements would substantially reduce horn use and its concomitant noise pollution. Each failure to file a Horn Incident Report within the requisite time period is punishable by a $250 fine. Now, Farber, June 15th? Did you or did you not file a Horn Incident Report?"

My eyes wander around the room. Although of course it's been there for the whole ten hours, I notice now for the first time a painting of a mallard duck on the wall above Lugo's desk. The painting is yellowed with age, and downright awful.

"Farber, are you aware that, according to current estimates, the Horn Honking Reduction Act of 2003 has caused an average nine percent decrease in noise pollution in major urban centers?"

I stare at the painting of the duck. The brushstrokes are crude, and the artist's complete failure to understand even the rudimentary concepts of basic color theory is alarming. It's possible it was painted by a dim four year old.

"That your duck painting?" I ask, motioning to the picture with a quick head swivel.

He ignores me and makes a notation of some sort on a sheaf of papers. "So, then, I will mark June 15th as a violation," he says, starting to close up the file.

I debate whether to say anything. If I point out the obvious mistake he's made, it could cause another interminable delay. On the other hand, if I can convince him that the horn engagement was reasonable, I might have some chance of getting out of the fine. I know I should just keep my mouth shut. In fact, I should have agreed to pay all the fines when I first walked into this hellhole ten hours ago. I don't know what compels me to speak, but here I am, opening my mouth, and the words come tumbling out.

"You forgot to look at the back of the pink form again. How many times must I remind you? My reflections are recorded in the appropriate subsection of the relevant document, as always."

"Oh, yeah, right," he says. He leafs through the paperwork until he finds the pink form labeled "Horn Incident Report." He looks over the basic data of the incident recorded on the front of the form and then turns the sheet over to read my reflections. "Mmmm, it says here that you engaged your horn three times on the afternoon of June 15th because you, and I quote, had to allocate the remains of the ham sandwich that had been provided by the Policy Bureau, unquote." He slams the folder down in front of him and glares at me. "Now, what the hell could that possibly mean?"

I have no idea. But under the regulations, if I can convince Lugo that my explanation was reasonable, then I avoid the fine. This is what's been taking so much time. He won't agree that an explanation is reasonable without probing every possibility, understanding every nuance. This can take hours. But I've successfully gotten out of three fines so far, and with my job situation as it is, I need the cash. For most of the other incidents, however, my reflections, ludicrous as they may have been, had provided me with some semblance of an argument. I've given myself very little to work with here.

"Well, umm, ehh," I begin. "You know, it's all very complicated, I was hungry, umm, you see, and there was this sandwich. Anyways, the Policy Bureau, you know, the uhh Governor's Mansion and such, well...."

Lugo is drilling holes in my head with his stare. I ramble on for several minutes, trying to salvage something from the murky language, but Lugo remains unmoved. He's heard a lot of suspicious crap from me today, and he's not buying my story at all. I should shut up, but I can't seem to let it go. The sweat is running down my spine in waves. The room is getting smaller.

I am enveloped by Lugo's mass. Suddenly and without explanation, I lunge across the tiny desk that separates us and thrust my fist deep into the folds of Lugo's belly flesh. Ignoring his screams, I pluck the dark purplish mass right off his skin and fall back to my side of the desk. I look into my fist and realize that it is indeed a mushroom that has been growing on Lugo's body. It is a small mushroom, sort of like a straw mushroom that you might find floating in an egg drop soup or a Thai hot and sour soup, or some other sort of soup.

"My mushroom! My mushroom!" Lugo squawks, as he leaps and flails around the tiny office. "You've taken my mushroom!"

I'm suddenly overcome by an overwhelming sense of guilt. What have I done here? Lugo is grasping his considerable belly and squealing. I look down at my palm once again and have no idea why I am holding this mushroom. It is not mine. I should give it back. I stand up, nearly whimpering myself, and hand the mushroom back over the desk towards my interrogator. "Here," I say, "take the mushroom." Before he can figure out what's happening, I fling the mushroom back at him. It bounces off his chest and falls to the floor. As Lugo precariously bends over to retrieve it, I turn and make for the door. They can fine me any amount they want, but I cannot stay in this room for one more moment.

IDENTITY

AM I A
MUFFIN
OR A
MUSHROOM

CRISIS

Three Screams

The Neo-Lamarckian studies his test-tubes and charts the data. Florescent cylinders illuminate him from above; below, ordered columns of figures march upon his cluttered workspace. A half-drunk Diet Coke provides the necessary companionship. This is his home, this Vancouver laboratory. The Neo-Lamarckian makes a notation in his tiny notebook and grins like a maniac. Thinking about Darwin, he feels his blood pressure rising, the vein in his forehead inflating dangerously. Transferring solutions, examining transformations, observing relationships, he works furiously, until the anger boils over. "Natural selection, my ass!" he screams, "Galapagos Finches, my hairy ass!!" but nobody hears him because it is 3 a.m. on a Saturday and the lab, save for himself, is empty.

In a small town near Omaha, The Stratego Player studies his remaining pieces and settles on his next move. With his left hand (always his left, though he is otherwise right-handed; Stratego players are second to none when it comes to superstition), he lifts a bomb, pretends to consider moving it one space forward, then replaces it in its original position before moving the adjacent Sergeant ("7") one space to the left. The idea, of course, is to trick the opponent, make her think the bomb is actually a movable piece. This move is his invention and the key to last year's national championship. By this season, however, the move has become old hat and fools nobody. "Pulling a Jackass?" asks his adversary in this quarterfinal match-up, invoking the common query now routinely uttered to ridicule the shopworn tactic. Thinking about his lackluster performance these last six months, The Stratego Player feels his blood pressure rising, the vein in his right temple inflating dangerously. His pimply adolescent opponent smirks and takes his bomb with her Miner ("8"). The Stratego Player is visibly shaken and performs poorly during the game's denouement, his defeat virtually assured by the loss of this last bomb. When his flag is finally taken, and his exit from the national tournament finalized, his anger boils over. "I need a new move," he screams, clearing with one sweep of his hand the rest of the board's red and blue pieces. "I need some new damned thing!!"

As the intruder ransacks the upstairs floors of his suburban Maryland home, The Lawyer struggles to free his hands from the coarse rope that binds them to his Princeton Class of '81 Chair. He and his wife look at each other from opposite sides of their ornately decorated living room. She too has been bound tightly to a chair; hers, however, boasts a Wellesley seal and is constructed from a lighter shade of wood. The intruder reappears at the foot of the staircase and flaunts his treasure. "My girlfriend will love this necklace," he says, swinging the string of brilliant sapphires around his head like a lasso. When the wife audibly groans, the intruder figures it is time to finish the job. Watching the intruder approach with butcher's knife drawn high, The Lawyer feels his heart racing, works his fingers desperately to free himself. When he realizes all is hopeless, his anger boils over. He turns to face his struggling wife and screams: "Goddamnit, how could you leave the door unlocked again? How many times have I told you? What's your problem?" And then it's lights out.

At The Lawyer's funeral, The Neo-Lamarckian and The Stratego Player pay their final respects to their brother, talk quietly about their childhood. The last time they saw each other was a half decade ago, at the side-by-side funeral that followed their parents' bizarre murder-suicide incident. Then, the media trucks outnumbered the mourners. Now, the graveyard is quiet and creepy. The service ends. The brothers embrace, take one last sad look around the cemetery, go their separate ways.

The Proofreader

Slouched over his poorly illuminated proofreading desk, Dunbar considered what a wretched, miserable, and altogether terrible day he was having. He had just finished three straight hours of proofreading a complicated article detailing the recent rise in osteopathic illness in the local Greentown area and was currently seeing double from the boring and irrelevant statistics that he had been required to verify. Dunbar hated statistics. He also hated his job. "Goddammit, I hate this job," he muttered as he took a sip of his now cold lemon tea. He grimaced as the citric acid inflamed the canker sore that had begun to fester on the inside of his lower lip. "Don't get me wrong. I love proofreading," he told himself. "If only I had something good to proofread, then I'd be as happy as a lark, whatever the hell that means." He turned his head back to the desk and began inspecting his newest piece of work, an article on overcrowding at the town zoo, when his boss, Mr. Rose, approached him from behind.

"Dunbar!" Mr. Rose wailed. "Under what conditions do we utilize a semicolon within a sentence?"

Dunbar was startled by this rude interruption and squirmed in his seat as he tried to recall the rules for semicolon usage. They escaped him for a moment, but soon he remembered the pertinent section in the English grammar textbook that he had unfailingly carried around throughout college. Within moments, Dunbar was able to recite from memory the exact rules governing semicolon use. "There are four situations in which a semicolon is used," he began. "First, to separate the clauses of a compound sentence having no coordinating conjunction. Second, to separate the clauses of a compound sentence containing internal punctuation. Third, to separate the elements of a series in which the items already contain commas, and fourth, to separate clauses of a compound sentence joined by a conjunctive adverb such as 'nonetheless' or 'therefore.'" He took a deep breath. "Is that right?"

"Yes, that's right, Dunbar!" thundered Mr. Rose. "Now why don't you tell me how come there's no semicolon in this sentence?!" He slammed down a copy of the "Animals Need Blood Too: Greentown Announces First Animal Blood Drive" article that Dunbar had been working on earlier in the day and pointed to the sentence in question. Dunbar looked at the sentence that Mr. Rose's chubby, hairy finger was pointing at. It read: "Dogs and cats are by far the most needy, nevertheless, other pets such as birds and lizards also occasionally require blood transfusions." Dunbar immediately realized his mistake, but he was far from surprised. He considered himself a damned good proofreader, but proofreading articles like this one was too much to ask from a professional like him. He vaguely remembered trying to pop his canker with his teeth while working on it.

"Well, Dunbar? Is there any good reason you can give me for screwing this up?" Mr. Rose demanded.

"Because you're wearing that hideous mustard-green shirt?" Dunbar thought.

"I don't know. I'm very sorry," Dunbar said. "I'll try to be a better proofreader in the future."

"You better be, if you want to remain affiliated with this local newspaper for any length of time," Mr. Rose said, and then he grabbed the article, spun around on his wingtip shoes, and left the room.

"What a bad man," Dunbar thought to himself as he took another agonizing sip of tea. Dunbar had been at the *Greentown Crow* now for four months and blamed the entire misfortune of his working experience on Mr. Rose. Dunbar felt that he was a promising young proofreader; after all, he had served as the head proofreader for his college newspaper, hadn't he? He simply needed a chance to sink his teeth into some real stories at the *Crow* to prove how good a proofreader he was. Then he was sure he could land a job at a major urban paper. Why did Mr. Rose hate him so much? Why was Mr. Rose giving him such a hard time? As he did every day, Dunbar once again concluded that Mr. Rose was a moron, and then he returned to his piece.

"Hey, why do you look so down today, Dunbar?" Blatz, one of Dunbar's senior colleagues, inquired. Blatz had just returned from lunch at the rib joint down on Murphy Avenue and was looking round and content. Dunbar had to admit that although Blatz got all of the good articles that Mr. Rose himself didn't get, and although he had no ambition whatsoever (he had worked at the *Crow* for twenty-five years), nevertheless, there was nothing really bad to say about him. In fact, Dunbar seriously respected Blatz's sobriety and moral character. Dunbar considered his own sole fault to be an occasional glass of sherry, but never, in all his time working at the paper, had he heard Blatz so much as mention alcohol. Every once in a while, Dunbar imagined that, by combining his own talent and hard work with Blatz's uprightness concerning liquor consumption, he could become an absolutely unstoppable proofreader.

"Oh, I just had a run-in with Mr. Rose," Dunbar replied.

"Another apostrophe problem?" Blatz asked with a chuckle, referring to an embarrassing event of the previous week.

"No—semicolons this time. I just can't concentrate on these irrelevant articles," Dunbar said, scratching his greasy head.

"Oh, it's not that bad. Things could be worse," Blatz urged with his characteristically blank but optimistic manner.

"That's easy for you to say!" Dunbar sat upright and exclaimed. "You get great articles to proofread. Just take today, for instance. While I sit here and read Marlteby's article on zoo overcrowding, you get to proofread Steiner's front page piece on bribery in the state legislature. If only you knew how much I wish I could be reading what you read."

"That's O.K., kid. Stick around here as long as I have, and you'll have all the front page pieces you want," Blatz retorted before walking back to his desk on the other side of the office.

Dunbar reclined in his chair, put his hands over his face, and contemplated with dread a twenty-five year stint at the *Greentown Crow*. He thought about staring at the same brown walls, the same faint, florescent overhead lighting, the same Mr. Rose, every weekday for twenty-five years. The picture seemed almost too bleak to bear. Dunbar considered getting up and quitting right then and there when Mr. Crenshaw, the Editor-in-Chief, came running frantically into the office with an article in his hand.

"Where the hell are the proofreaders? I need a proofreader on the double!" he yelled.

Blatz turned to Crenshaw from his stooped-over position at the water dispenser where he had ventured to get a cup of hot water. "I'm a proofreader," he said. "Maybe you recognize me from the twenty-five years of service I've put in here? What can I do for you?"

Crenshaw looked quizzically at Blatz, obviously unable to remember who the portly man was. "We have a huge story that just came in about an hour ago," he said. "I want to get it in the afternoon edition so I need it proofread right away. Mr. Rose is at the sandwich shop getting a turkey sandwich, I'm not familiar with the intricacies of newspaper grammar, and I'm sure that I don't recognize a single one of you. So what the hell am I gonna do?"

Dunbar saw his chance at once. "I'll take it, sir. I'll be glad to take it." He leapt up and ran over to where Crenshaw was standing. "I'm a proofreader, and a damned good one at that. I welcome the opportunity to proofread an important article." Dunbar looked back at Blatz to see if he would object to the suggestion, but Blatz had an understanding look on his face and even gave Dunbar a slight wink. "You've got to let me have the article, Mr. Crenshaw. You've just got to," Dunbar insisted, as he grabbed the article out of Crenshaw's hand.

"Well...." Crenshaw considered Dunbar's young and enthusiastic face. "I don't have any idea who you are, and there's nothing in my past experience I can use to understand what the hell you're so excited about, but I don't see any reason why you shouldn't proofread the story if you want to proofread the story. You did say that you're a proofreader, didn't you?"

"Yes, sir. One of the world's best."

"In that case, have it on my desk in one hour."

"Yes, sir!"

Newly energized, Dunbar hurried back to his desk to begin work on the new project. He settled into his metal chair and placed the article down on the proofreading table. For the first time in months, he felt like he was doing something valuable with his time. Eagerly, he began surveying the contents of the piece.

"Hmmm. A crime story," he thought.

The article concerned a kidnapping that had taken place earlier in the day. A student at Greentown University named Scott Robinson had apparently lost control after learning that he had failed to gain acceptance to the Molecular Biology Department's Ph.D. program. Robinson, who was described by acquaintances as clearly psychotic and absolutely unable to understand even the most basic concepts of molecular biology, had stormed into the department offices and taken the Chairman, Professor Glen Davis, hostage at about 10:00 a.m. Robinson, in an effort to prove that he was "smart enough to get a degree from Harvard, never mind dumb-ass Greentown University," had demanded that Harvard deliver him a full-fledged diploma within the next twenty-four hours or else he would kill Davis. Harvard administrators, perplexed by the odd demand, announced that giving Robinson a diploma was an utter impossibility, as he had not even satisfactorily completed the Core Curriculum requirement. Thus, the situation was at a standstill, and Greentown police, having never before faced a situation more dangerous than the freak child-biting incident that had occurred outside the grizzly bear cage at the overcrowded Greentown Zoo the August before last, were rendered entirely impotent by the whole affair.

Dunbar dove into his proofreading job with relish. He fixed several misplaced colons, adjusted numerous spelling mistakes, and scratched out a superfluous hyphen. He even took the liberty of fixing up a couple of dangling modifiers. When he was in college, Dunbar had often argued for the expansion of the proofreader's role into the area of editing; once, in a fit of passion, he had even been compelled to claim in a paper that: "With the advent of a new breed of proofreader, the editor might someday become entirely obsolete. At least we can only hope so!" Dunbar was definitely not going to pass up such a splendid opportunity to do a little editing. Indeed, Dunbar was as happy as he had been in months. He was whistling "Oh, Suzanna" and joyfully slashing, erasing, and crossing things out when a livid Mr. Rose came barging into the back office, bits of turkey dangling from his prickly mustache.

"Dunbar! What the hell do you think you're doing?" he yelled.

Suddenly returned to a state of insignificance, Dunbar turned around and faced Mr. Rose with a quivering lower lip.

"Well? Are you proofreading that kidnapping story or what?" Rose repeated.

"I guess so," Dunbar squealed.

"Not any more you're not! Who do you think you are, talking Mr. Crenshaw into letting you proofread an important article? Don't you know by now that you're not qualified to be proofreading such a prominent news item? Now, suppress those dreams of glory you're always howling about and get back to that zoo-overcrowding piece for Christ's sake. Section D, page 26 is dying from empty space."

"But...I'm not even finished."

"You're finished now, Dunbar," Rose screamed as he grabbed the article and left the office.

Crestfallen, Dunbar slowly returned his attention to the zoo piece and halfheartedly proofread it until 4:30, when he put on his brown coat and his brown hat and shuffled off to the bus which delivered him to his dark and depressing home.

The next morning, when Dunbar awoke from habit at 7:30, he decided that he absolutely could not go to work after the previous day's humiliation. He got up, fixed himself some corn flakes, and sat down at his white, crumb-covered kitchen table. The weather outside was miserable. Between spoonfuls of cereal, Dunbar considered what he could do to brighten the day. After a bit of deliberation he decided to listen to the radio. He got up and turned on his favorite AM station. The lead news story was coming to the very end.

"To repeat: This morning, two Greentown citizens, Scott Robinson and Glen Davis, lie dead, and one sorry, pathetic proofreader is being asked to shoulder every last drop of the blame. We will have more on this story later as additional information becomes available. WNUS newstime is 8:00, and I'm John McFee...." The announcer's voice faded away as Dunbar tried to process the information he had just heard. "Did they say a proofreader was to blame? For two deaths? What did they mean?" Dunbar turned these questions over in his groggy brain as he quickly shoveled the soggy cereal down his throat. Realizing suddenly that something important might be going on at the newspaper office, Dunbar decided that he had better get there as soon as possible. He ran into his cluttered bedroom, threw on a pair of unlaundered pants, a soiled shirt, and his shoes, and ran out the front door to catch the eight o'clock bus.

When Dunbar arrived at the *Greentown Crow* building, he was met by a roomful of frightened and inquisitive faces. Luckily, Mr. Rose had not seen him entering the office, so Dunbar had some time to find out what was going on from Blatz. Quickly, he approached Blatz's desk.

"Blatz, what's going on?" Everyone in the office looks like they've seen a ghost, and I heard something on the news about some deaths and a proofreader and...."

"Read the fourth paragraph," Blatz said coolly as he handed Dunbar a folded up copy of yesterday afternoon's newspaper.

Dunbar immediately recognized the kidnapping article that he had been working on the day before. After gaining his bearings by reviewing the first three quite well-proofread paragraphs, Dunbar turned his attention to the fourth. At first, he could find nothing noteworthy, but after a couple of times through, he realized the problem. It was in the final sentence, which read, "According to sources close to the kidnapper, Robinson had decided to take the hostage and demand the Harvard diploma when he was humiliatingly denied admission to grade school."

"Uh oh," Dunbar thought.

"GRADE SCHOOL?! GRADE SCHOOL?! Where's that twirpy Dunbar and his crappy little proofreading pencil? I'll shove it right through his heart," Mr. Rose roared as he came barreling towards the back office.

There was no time to hide, so Dunbar quickly prepared himself for the worst of disasters.

"There you are, Dunbar, you goddamned proofreader!" Mr. Rose screeched as he burst into the room brandishing the offending story. "What possible explanation can you conceivably offer to explain how you allowed this article to say 'grade school' instead of 'grad school'? What fathomable excuse could you possibly fabricate to allow me to explain to every national newspaper and television station in the country that it wasn't our fault that a freaked out lunatic who went insane when he couldn't get into a Ph.D. program decided to kill himself and a university professor because he read in our newspaper that he wasn't even smart enough to get into the third grade?"

"Uhhh..." Dunbar retorted.

"'Uhhh'? Is that what I should tell the staff of *Dateline* when they ask me to explain why we're responsible for the first murder in Greentown history? 'Well, that's an interesting question, that question you have about our responsibility for the murder. In response, I'd like to say *uhhhh*.' Seems like a bad idea, Dunbar. Got any other ideas?" Mr. Rose stared openmouthed at Dunbar for an uncomfortable couple of moments before Blatz spoke out suddenly in Dunbar's defense.

"Maybe if you had let him finish proofreading the article instead of running in here all turkey-faced and stealing it from him, there would have been no mistake."

"Are you saying this is my fault?" Mr. Rose blurted.

"Well, you did storm in here and grab the article away from Dunbar while he was still working on it."

Mr. Rose made a concerted effort not to kill Blatz. He paused to recover his composure before carefully laying out his position. "I may have stolen it away from him," he said, "but Dunbar anointed himself head proofreader for the piece. He proofread the thing for an hour and a half, and therefore he must be considered responsible for the goddamned murder that transpired due to his incompetency!"

"But don't you think that by stealing the article away from him, you thereby anointed yourself the head proofreader for the piece?" Blatz responded.

Mr. Rose mulled over Blatz's argument carefully. "Don't think that you can get your little pal Dunbar out of trouble with your convoluted logic, Mr. Blatz. I'm far too smart for that sort of trick," he said, grinning stupidly.

"Yes, I suppose you are, Mr. Rose."

"Furthermore, I'm the boss, and don't think for two minutes that I don't know about your two martini lunches."

Dunbar, who had been silent throughout the argument, now looked at Blatz with surprise. "What two martini lunches?" he thought.

Blatz pounded the water dispenser with his fist. "You're being entirely unreasonable, Rose. Trying to pin responsibility for a murder-suicide on a proofreader who wasn't even responsible for proofreading the article you erroneously think is the cause of the murder-suicide is completely outrageous," Blatz barked. Having vented the last of his dissent, he threw his hands up in the air and returned to his desk, where he had been in the process of proofreading an article on the city gasoline tax.

Mr. Rose, who was completely baffled by Blatz's uprising, began pacing around the office. Apart from Blatz, everyone else in the office was silent and staring at Mr. Rose and Dunbar. Dunbar, for his part, was standing motionless in the center of the room. He was licking his canker and thinking about everything that had been happening to him. He honestly could not remember whether he had proofread the "grade" or not, but he was fairly sure that he must not have, since he would never make that egregious an error in proofreading a document. Nevertheless, everyone but Blatz seemed to think it was his fault, and now it turned out that Blatz was a drunk who imbibed martinis like they were lemonades. Who was anybody to say what was true and what was not true? If Blatz could guzzle gin and olives to wash down his pork ribs, then maybe Mr. Rose was right, and he really did screw up the piece. Maybe he *was* responsible for the murder, although that idea still seemed rather inconceivable. And what did responsibility mean, anyway? Just because Blatz lapped up vermouth like a fish, did that give Mr. Rose the right to yell at him in front of all these people? Who the hell knew? Dunbar continued to stand silently, wondering about all these possibilities when Mr. Rose, on the verge of exploding with anger, suddenly turned on his heels and addressed him directly.

"Well, Dunbar? We've heard what Blatz thinks. What do *you* have to say about the whole matter? Are you going to accept responsibility for your actions or not?"

Dunbar considered the question dumbly for a few moments. "Well, I have no idea why I should accept responsibility, but ... of course I will," he said, and Mr. Rose lurched off to his office to begin preparing Dunbar's pink slip.

You Are Not Tu Fu

Yóu, my friend, are not Tu Fu.

Why you think you are Tu Fu is a mystery on the scale of Deep Throat's identity, the location of Hoffa's corpse. It is a topic that Melanie, Carney, and I discuss endlessly over green tea and cigarettes, with little progress. Figuring you out is like playing catch with sawdust.

Alone, Melanie thinks about the events of recent days and feels tears welling beneath puffy lids. She wonders what, if any, are the limits on these sorts of shenanigans? Christmas was so long ago, but your gift hat remains in her front pocket burning holes.

In Carney's apartment, shots of vodka are consumed, advertisements criticized at length. Carney finds the incessant Toyota commercials particularly insipid; Melanie suggests the invention of the "T-Chip" to block all such ads. Carney downs another shot of Ketel One and researches patent applications on the web. Melanie is trained in Excel, so her job is to run the numbers. Hours go by before anyone realizes the technology is out of reach. By then the vodka is gone, and they have started in on the dusty bottle of cheap bourbon. The night ends when Melanie declines Carney's advances. He is lovely and delightful aplenty, she says, but she is not ready. Not even close. This too, you have ruined. Ruined, you scoundrel!

To reiterate: You are not Tu Fu.

You are not a famous T'ang Dynasty poet.

You were not born in 712 A.D.

You did not grow up in Shanxi province.

You did not write a poem called "On Seeing a Painting of Horses by General Zao Pa At Secretary Wei Feng's House" (Or rather, you did write such a poem, largely plagiarized and inferior.)

You, perhaps most significantly, are not known for your incomparable honesty.

When Melanie arrives at my apartment, I am organizing my collection of cowry shells and daydreaming about Nova Scotia's rugged coastline. Melanie has come directly from Carney's, where she has spent a fitful night on an uncomfortable couch in a rapidly spinning living room. I offer her an extra toothbrush so she can clean up, but she chooses a beer instead despite the early hour. She has always been fascinated by my shell collection, and when she places a particularly large tiger-striped piece to her ear I know it is in hopes of hearing the South China Sea. This is the place to which you have fled with such short notice, settling in a bustling oceanside town with a relaxed tax structure intended to lure investment from overseas. I tell her that the sea one hears in a shell is inchoate, no specific ocean in particular, but my explanation drifts off unheeded into the room like wisps of smoke from an extinguished candle. I stop speaking and offer Melanie a tissue, which, unlike the toothbrush, she accepts without hesitation.

Here's a little quiz for you:

Q: Were you captured in the mid-750s by an army under the control of rebellious central Asian general An Lu-shan and brought to the capital of Ch'ang-an, where you penned a poem entitled "Looking at the Springtime"?

A: No.

As always, I am called upon to interpret your actions but have nothing to offer. We are old pals, friendship stretching back to our days together in the high school drama club. You excelled on stage, I worked the lights. Back then I could illuminate you, but no longer. Melanie asks my advice; I shrug my shoulders. She wonders whether she should get her own ticket to the Middle Kingdom; I don't know what to say. Even famous Chinese poets have to come home sometime, I offer, but I really, honestly don't know if that is true.

"I Didn't Come Out Too Good"

Acknowledgments

The author would like to send out humongously gigantic thanks to Alan Childress and Michele Veade of the awesome QP Books, without whom this book simply would not exist; to Dave Croy, artist extraordinaire, without whom the magnificent cover of this book would not exist; and to Erin Cox, publicity guru, without whom nobody would know that this book exists.

About the author

Jay Wexler is a law professor at Boston University, a former law clerk to Justice Ruth Bader Ginsburg, and the author of two books of non-fiction: *Holy Hullabaloos: A Road Trip to the Battlegrounds of the Church/State Wars*, and *The Odd Clauses: Understanding the Constitution Through Ten of its Most Curious Provisions*, both published by Beacon Press in Boston. In addition to many scholarly works, Wexler has published nearly fifty essays, stories, humor pieces, and reviews in places like *The Boston Globe*, *McSweeney's Internet Tendency*, *Mental Floss*, *Monkeybicycle*, *Opium*, and *Spy*. He lives with his wife and son in Boston's Leather District, where he is hard at work on, among other things, a novel involving Ed Tuttle.

Photo by Steve Lowther, taken at Malaprop's Bookstore in Asheville, North Carolina

Visit us at *www.qpbooks.com.*

Made in the USA
Charleston, SC
01 August 2012